Hope for Garbage

ALEX TULLY

Cover Art by Ana Grigoriu

Copyright © 2014 Alex Tully

ISBN-10: 0692024832

ISBN-13: 978-0-692-02483-6

For my family

When the world says, "Give up,"

Hope whispers, "Try it one more time."

~Anonymous

CHAPTER 1

Trevor McNulty cleared his throat and leaned forward in his chair. "Kleenex," he said, ending the silence.

Dr. Fisher looked up, a hint of surprise on her face, "Do you need a tissue?"

"No," he said. "At our first session, you asked me what I remembered about my mom. That's what I remember—kleenex."

The doctor narrowed her eyes at him, "Can you elaborate for me?"

This was their fifth session together, but the first time he had spoken a word. "See, she had this germ phobia thing. Every time she touched something she had to use a kleenex. And I mean everything. If she touched, I don't know…a bar of soap, she'd still have to use a kleenex."

Trevor scanned the small square room for the hundredth time. With nothing but empty beige walls and a potted rubber tree in one corner, the surroundings couldn't be more mind-numbing.

In fact, the only thing worth looking at was Dr. Fisher. She sat across from him in her oversized leather chair, writing diligently in her notepad. He had to give her credit. She had shown an impressive amount of patience.

Before agreeing to these sessions, Trevor had researched all of the doctors in the provider directory. If he had to be stuck in a small room with someone, for any length of time, a fat middle-aged bald man was not an option.

And it was no contest. Dr. Fisher was by far, the best-looking doctor at the Beaumont Health Center—or as he liked to call it, the Crazy Kids Center. She was probably in her thirties, with wavy blond hair that she constantly tucked behind her right ear. She had green eyes, and from the little bit he could see, a nice body. But she left a lot to the imagination in her usual black pantsuit and boring flat loafers. Would it kill her to wear a skirt once in a while?

"Trevor? You were saying?"

He quickly focused his attention back to Dr. Fisher's face, "Uh, yeah. At first she used those gloves. You know, the latex ones, like the kind they use in hospitals. But that didn't last long. They got too expensive, so she moved on to Kleenex." He wiped his hands on his jeans, "Weird, huh?"

Raindrops began pelting the side of the lone window. The sky quickly turned from a dreary white to an ominous gray. "Looks like we're getting a pretty nasty storm." He could really use a diversion right about now.

Dr. Fisher glanced at the window. "So you must have had a very clean home then," she said, ignoring his attempt at small talk.

For some reason this struck a nerve and he almost vaulted out of his chair, "Clean? Hell no! See that's what's so screwed up. Mom wouldn't clean anything, because in order to clean, you actually have to touch things."

His heart started racing. He never talked about Mom. Ever. "No, she wouldn't touch anything. The house was filthy. Piles of kleenex everywhere and crap all over the place. Truly, it was a dump."

As he sat back down, his gaze remained fixed on the black clouds moving across the sky. His unruly left eyelid twitched, "I think I was about seven or eight when I started doing the cleaning, and pretty much everything else." He took a deep breath. That was it—he was done talking.

But Dr. Fisher wasn't done. "That must have been hard on you, taking over the household responsibilities."

Here it comes. Now she was delving into the touchy-feely bullshit. *How did it make you feel Trevor?*

The dreaded sensations of anxiety rushed in. Somewhere deep inside him, the indescribable hot feeling erupted and quickly spread throughout his body. Beads of perspiration rose to the surface, breaking through his skin and covering him with a layer of sweat. He felt lightheaded—he needed some air—he needed to get the hell out of there.

"Trevor, are you okay?"

His legs trembled beneath him as he slowly got up from his chair, "You know what...I got this thing I forgot about. I have to go."

He hurried out of the office and didn't look back. This session was over.

***

Sucking in the cold damp air, Trevor closed his eyes and tried to breathe, "Pull yourself together Trevor!"

Deep breath in, deep breath out...

He finally steadied himself, got on his bike, and started the long ride home to Westwood. As if things could get any worse, the rain had turned into what meteorologists liked to call a "wintery mix." This was typical springtime weather for Cleveland—shitty. The brutal winter had done its damage to the asphalt roads, and slush-filled pot holes littered the street like landmines. Not a good day for a bike ride. Not like he had a choice.

Westwood was on the southwest edge of the city. A true blue-collar town, it was home to mostly middle-class families trying to pay the bills. It was also a hodge-podge of different ethnic groups, filled with Irish pubs, Italian pizzerias and Polish pierogi shops. Endless rows of 1950s bungalows lined the streets. Everyone drove American cars and everyone drank American beer.

He pulled his sweatshirt hood tighter, trying to shield his face from the stinging raindrops. His cheeks were burning, his fingers were numb, and his feet were soaked inside his Converse high-tops. He was cursing Mr.T.

Trevor wished he could skip these sessions with Dr. Fisher and just pretend to go. Been there, done that. It didn't work. Mr.T obviously had connections at the Crazy Kids Center. He knew exactly when Trevor got there and exactly when he made his exit. If Trevor didn't show, the clever old bird knew. Yeah, this was all part of their deal. He had made a promise to Mr.T, and now he had to stick to it.

As much as he hated the freezing rain, the cold air always helped to ease his anxiety. His appetite had come back in full force and his stomach rumbled at the thought of food. He hadn't eaten anything since that pathetic excuse for a veggie pizza at lunch.

He pedaled his bike down Canal Street into the center of town. Downtown Westwood wasn't much to look at, but it did have some of the best places to eat. One of his favorites was Sorak's Hungarian Diner and it was only a block away.

As he turned the corner, he could almost smell the cabbage and noodles wafting through the air. He loved those thick pieces of dough, hand-rolled as wide as a pencil, fried up with cabbage and tons of real butter. A little sour cream on the side and there was nothing better, especially on a day like today.

He parked his bike and entered the crowded diner. A gush of warm air and the aroma of fried onions greeted him at the door. He looked over at his favorite booth by the corner window. Not surprisingly it was occupied by an old couple, so he took a seat at the counter. Some might call him a regular, but he definitely didn't come here for the conversation.

Carol, the owner of the place, walked over. She was a short, chubby lady with shiny white dentures that looked way too big for her mouth. Her gray curly hair was smashed down under her Cleveland Indians hat.

"You want the usual honey?" she asked in her friendly drawl.

"Please," he looked down at the tattered placemat in front of him.

As she went behind the swinging doors into the kitchen, Trevor glanced around the diner. Probably not one person under the age of sixty. He would guess that most of them grew up on this kind of food. Not him. Home-cooked meals weren't Mom's thing. Cooking was something normal moms did.

In five minutes Carol was back with a heaping plate of cabbage and noodles and a tall glass of milk. She slid the check under his plate. Scribbled across the front in green marker, was *$3.50* and a big smiley face.

The first time Trevor came into the diner, she kept insisting the meal was on the house. He wasn't sure if she pitied him for his infamous past, or simply because he was dirt poor. The reason didn't matter; it pissed him off. They argued back and forth until Carol finally gave in and took his five dollars.

He took a huge bite, closed his eyes, and sighed. Savoring the buttery noodles, his shoulders relaxed and he sank deeper into his bar stool. Heaven.

"So how's it going Trevor?" Carol asked loudly, startling him out of his fleeting bliss. He stopped chewing and opened his eyes. This was the first time Carol had said anything to him other than 'The usual honey?'

He swallowed, "Uh, fine."

As she leaned over the counter, the smell of old-lady perfume, mixed with a hint of moth balls, hit him hard in the face. "Hey, I wanted to ask you—you live next door to Tom Tyminski don't you?"

Trevor had no idea how she knew this, and he wasn't sure he wanted to know. "Yeah." It was strange hearing Mr.T being called by his first name, "Mr.Tyminski. I live by him."

She nudged herself even closer to him, her elbows and huge breasts resting comfortably in front of his plate. Trevor immediately sat back and upright in his stool. She was one of those people who had zero understanding of personal space.

"See, I knew Tom back in high school. We actually went on a date once, to the drive-in. But everyone knew he was crazy about Maddie." Carol stopped there, staring out over Trevor's shoulder. "That was Tom's wife. She was a beautiful lady. She passed in '96 I think. Gosh, has it been that long? Terrible tragedy…" she trailed off, her eyes wide.

Trevor turned around and looked over his shoulder, just to make sure there wasn't a fire outside or something.

Carol finally blinked and focused her eyes on him again. "Anyway, can you tell him Carol Sorak said 'Hi'? Tell him to come in for lunch sometime so we can catch up. I'd love to see him."

Trevor forced a weak smile, "Yeah, I can do that I guess." He just wanted to eat before the noodles got cold. He took another hefty mouthful.

As she walked back to the kitchen, Carol called over her shoulder, "And you make sure to tell him—the noodles are on me."

A very disturbing visual popped into Trevor's head, and he pushed his plate away. He had suddenly lost his appetite.

CHAPTER 2

Tom Tyminski sat in the living room of his modest two-bedroom ranch watching the Weather Channel. After seventy plus years, not much on television held his interest anymore. The five-day forecast said warmer weather for tomorrow, but for the rest of today it would be cold and rainy. He felt a little sorry for Trevor having to ride his bike through it. But there was one thing Tom was certain of—the kid was not a sissy.

He slowly got up out of his La-Z-Boy and plodded over to the kitchen. Getting old was a bitch, no way to sugar-coat it. He opened the freezer and surveyed the inside as if something new might magically appear. Instead, the usual stack of orange rectangular boxes filled the frozen space: Stouffer's meat lasagna, pot-pie and

Salisbury steak. "What do you think Jip? I'm thinking the pot-pie is looking appetizing."

Tom looked down at Trevor's scruffy little mutt. He had offered to watch the dog while the kid was at school. No reason why they should both be alone all day—might as well keep each other company.

Jip wasn't going to win any best-in-show ribbons. His matted brown hair, pointy ears, and sad eyes gave him a pitiful appearance. Trevor thought he was a mix of shepherd and chow; Tom thought Border terrier. It didn't really matter because they both loved the little guy. Jip was the reason the two of them became friends in the first place.

Four years ago, Trevor had moved in next door. Tom heard all of the gossip about the boy at church. After nine o'clock mass, the whispers would go back and forth over coffee and donuts in the St. Pat's gym. "Did you hear about that crazy McNulty lady? Her boy is coming to live with relatives, right here in Westwood." Tom didn't pay much attention. He had seen the story on the news like everyone else.

Trevor's uncle lived next door. Gary McNulty was a jackass. There was no tip-toeing around it. After living next to him for twenty years, Tom picked up on things. Their houses were a little more than arms-length apart. The only thing separating them was a long gravel driveway and a broken chain-link fence. Even when he tried to avoid it, Tom saw and heard things he'd wished he hadn't.

After Trevor moved into the place, it was a few months before Tom even saw the boy. The kid never seemed to come out of the house. Finally, when winter came, and two feet of snow blanketed the ground, he started making regular appearances. Trevor would trudge through the snowy backyard and disappear into the dilapidated garage along their back property line. Tom didn't know how the kid managed not to freeze to death. The nights came early in the winter, and by six o'clock it was pitch black. A dim light glowed in the small window of the garage, and it never went out before nine.

One evening Tom was in his backyard filling up his bird feeder, when he heard what sounded like whimpering. In the boxwoods that ran along the back of his yard, he found a dog. The mutt was hiding under some low branches looking half-starved, and he wasn't wearing a collar. Tom had never seen the dog before and thought maybe it could be the kid's. When he saw the light go on in the garage, he walked over and knocked.

A minute probably passed before the door slowly creaked open. A skinny kid with big brown eyes and wavy brown hair stood on the inside. He was wearing a shoddy wool coat that hung to his knees—most likely a hand-me-down from his uncle. The boy was thirteen at the time, but looked even younger.

Tom smiled, "Hi, I'm Mr.Tyminski. I live next door." He gestured over to the back of his house with his free hand. The kid stared at him like he was speaking Chinese. "I was wondering if this dog was yours. He was hiding in my backyard."

"Uh, hi...I'm Trevor." The boy's face softened as his eyes focused on the pooch. "No, he's not mine, but I can take him. I mean, if he needs a place to stay, I could definitely take him."

Tom hesitated, studying the young boy in front of him. The dog did seem to be in pretty bad shape and he highly doubted anyone would come to claim him. At the very least, the mutt needed temporary shelter. It was frigid outside and more snow was on the way.

Trevor's eyes were pleading. "I'll take really good care of him."

Tom looked down at the shivering bundle of fur. "Do you think it will be okay with your uncle?"

The kid frowned, "He's never home. He wouldn't even notice."

"Well, do you have money for dog food?" Tom asked, already knowing the answer.

The enthusiasm in Trevor's face disappeared, and Tom felt a pang of pity for the boy. Of course Tom could buy the dog food on his own, but he had a better idea. "You know, I can't do a lot of things I used to be able to do. Things like shoveling snow and mowing the grass. How about you do some odd jobs around my house, and I can give you some money for dog food. I could really use the help. See, it goes both ways. I do something for you, and you do something for me."

The kid nodded enthusiastically and smiled for the first time, "Yes. I can do that stuff for you, for sure."

And just like that, Tom handed the dog over. As Trevor wrapped the mutt up in his oversized wool sleeves, Tom walked away from the garage and headed home. Smiling in the cold night air, he recited a quote from one of his favorite movies out loud, "I think this is the beginning of a beautiful friendship."

"Jip!" The reminiscing was over. Tom's thoughts were interrupted by a loud yell from outside, "Jip!" Then came a shrill whistle, and Jip's ears instantly shot up. Tail wagging, the dog ran to the back door and began barking.

Tom looked out the kitchen window. Trevor was running through the backyard, yelling for his dog. The kid burst through the back door, soaking wet and out of breath. He stood in the doorway, hunched over with his hands on his knees. Rain water dripped from his saturated clothes, quickly forming little puddles on the linoleum floor. He did not look happy.

"Wow Mr.T this was a great day for a bike ride" he said. "I think I'll be able to feel my fingers again in a few hours." Trevor picked up Jip and the dog began licking his face like it was a slab of bacon.

Trevor took off his wet socks and shoes and Tom quickly walked over and picked them up, "Oh quit your whining. It's not that bad. You'll defrost. Here, take off that shirt too. You can wear one of mine." Then he added, "Keep your skivvies on though—I'm not giving you those."

Tom went down to the basement and threw the kid's clothes in the dryer. When he came back up, Trevor was lying on the couch wearing one of Tom's favorite t-shirts. It was black with white lettering across the front that said

'My wild oats have turned to shredded wheat'. Jip was curled up next to him and the television was off.

Tom took a seat in his La-Z-Boy and put his feet up. Sadly, one trip up the basement stairs was enough to aggravate his bunions. "So how did it go?" he asked.

Trevor's eyes were closed, "Same as always…it was fine."

"What color was she wearing today?" Tom provoked.

"Black. It's always something exciting like brown or black."

At least the kid had a sense of humor. Tom smiled as they sat together in the quiet room. Other than Jip's panting, the ticking of the grandfather clock was the only sound. Outside noises and distractions weren't needed when they were together. Neither of them were big fans of TV, and Trevor didn't have any of those high-tech gadgets all the kids were carrying around these days. Tom did get the kid a basic cell phone—that was a necessity. But, talk, or no talk, they were completely comfortable just 'being' with each other.

This after-school routine had pretty much stayed the same over the last couple of years. Trevor seemed to avoid the inside of his uncle's house as much as possible. The kid would probably go work in his garage until dinner time. Then he would come back to Tom's for a lowly frozen dinner, usually macaroni and cheese. Neither of them had any desire to cook, no matter how many orange boxes they went through in a week. After dinner, the kid would head back over to his garage and work into the night. And when Tom went to bed, he would always see the light from the garage window, glowing in the darkness.

"Hey, I met an old friend of yours today. I think her name is Carol—at Sorak's diner. She told me to say 'Hi' and tell you to stop by sometime. She's, uh…interesting."

Tom remembered her. He hadn't seen Carol Sorak in a long time, not since Maddie's funeral. "Yeah I did some work for Carol at the diner a few times, years ago. She had an old fryer that kept breaking down." Tom was an electrician by trade and had learned to fix almost anything through the years.

"Well, she said you guys dated in high school," Trevor teased.

Tom felt his face getting hot. "What? No, we went on a date once I think. Maybe the drive-in? Geez, I can't remember. That was over fifty years ago!" He could hear the kid snickering over on the couch. "Dated my ass…" he muttered. "Oh, so now you're Carol's gossip buddy, huh?"

Trevor laughed, "No! Are you kidding me? I just went in there for cabbage and noodles and she started talking to me like I was her best friend or something. She told me—to tell you—to come to the diner. And I quote, 'the noodles are on her'."

Tom ignored the kid's attempt at crude humor. "And you didn't bring me any!" His eyes widened at the mere mention of real food. "Now we have to eat that

TV-dinner crap." What he wouldn't give for a home-cooked meal.

"Well, you weren't very high on my favorite's list when I was riding home from the Crazy Kids Center."

Tom tried to suppress a laugh. "Trevor, please don't call it that."

"Hey, just telling it like it is."

"It's just a place kids can go to talk about their problems. A lot of kids. And they're just like you. You don't think *you're* crazy, do you?"

Trevor got up from the couch. "You know what Mr.T? I'm seventeen and my best friend is like seventy. Maybe I am crazy," he walked toward the back door with Jip at his heels. "See ya Mr.T. I'm going to work!"

"See you later kid!" Tom called after him. He smiled as he thought about what the kid had just said—*his best friend*. He reclined in his chair and closed his eyes. He would be dozing in no time.

CHAPTER 3

The nightmare was always the same. Trevor flew over a large grassy field, frantically flapping his arms, trying to stay up in the air. A man dressed in black ran on the ground below him, reaching up for him, trying to catch him. Every time Trevor stopped flapping his arms, he fell closer to the man's clutches.

His arms were so tired. He couldn't keep this up much longer. As he fell closer to the ground, he could hear the man-in-black singing. Trevor couldn't make out the song at first, but then he recognized the familiar tune: "Welcome to the new age…to the new age…Welcome to the new age…"

Trevor sat up in a cold sweat. His cell phone was buzzing and playing the "Radioactive" ringtone. He looked over at the red numbers glowing on the clock—5:47 a.m. Flashing on his cell phone was the name

17

FRANK. He flipped it open, "Jesus Frank, why are you calling me at five in the morning?"

"I know, sorry kid. I had to call before my shift starts. But you'll be thanking me later."

Trevor yawned, "OK, what do you got?"

There was excitement in Frank's voice, "Honda HRX, really nice. It won't be out there long. You've got to snatch it up."

Trevor threw off his cover and sat up on the edge of the bed, "Where?"

"Well that's the thing. It's up in Harbor Village, on Lakeside Avenue."

Harbor Village was one of the wealthiest suburbs outside of Cleveland. It was also a place where residents weren't fond of outsiders snooping around. He sighed, "Frank, you know I can't go up there. Uncle Gary will kick my ass."

"Kid, I'm telling you it'll be worth it. He doesn't have to know where you got it."

Trevor was thinking it through. He wasn't physically afraid of his uncle. The fat slob wouldn't stand a chance against him in a fair fight. But he didn't like the idea of losing the roof over his head either. Still, these opportunities didn't come around very often...

"Hey kid, I've got to get to work." Frank sounded impatient, "Are you interested, or should I make some other calls?"

He knew he might regret this. "Give me the address."

***

As quietly as he could, Trevor took a quick shower and got dressed. The last thing he wanted to do was wake up Uncle Gary. He threw on his usual outfit of Levi's and a hooded sweatshirt and tip-toed down the stairs. An atomic bomb probably wouldn't be enough to wake his uncle, but Trevor didn't want to take any chances.

He opened the back door and let Jip out. It was supposed to be in the fifties today with lots of sun—balmy for May. And thanks to Frank, he now had a jump on a hot lead. Maybe today would shape up to be pretty decent.

While Jip burned another yellow spot in the grass, Trevor grabbed a granola bar and a Pepsi. The clock on the microwave showed 6:18. It was going to be close, but he should be able to make it to Harbor Village and back by 7:30. He had to leave now and he had to be fast. There'd be hell to pay if he didn't get Uncle Gary's truck back in time.

Grabbing the keys off the kitchen counter, he said goodbye to Jip and hurried out the back door. He got into the truck and headed north.

The posh suburb of Harbor Village bordered a three mile stretch of Lake Erie coastline. It was a picturesque wooded community, filled with sprawling houses, quaint shops, and plenty of rich people. Just thinking about the place made Trevor cringe.

As he reached Lake Avenue, he began looking for the address Frank had given him. The front yards of most lakefront mansions were vast, and the homes sat far back from the street. Address plaques were usually posted somewhere along the road—on a gate, a boulder, or a post.

The sun hadn't risen yet, and Trevor's eyes strained in the darkness as he scanned the address numbers. He drove along the street slowly, as Uncle Gary's muffler spewed exhaust fumes over the perfectly manicured lawns. He could only hope he wouldn't draw attention.

Finally, he came to a large statue of a swan sitting atop an ornate stone pillar. The numbers 12399 were engraved below the swan. This was it. As he expected, the home was set far back and hidden by an expanse of towering oak trees. He couldn't see what the house looked like, but he really didn't need to. All he cared about was the prize.

The aging pick-up slowed along the curb to a stop. No one in sight. Trevor got out and hurried across the tree lawn, avoiding the dim glow of an overhead street light. As he approached the end of the driveway he stopped dead in his tracks.

At the top of the drive, a car door slammed and an engine suddenly came to life. Bright red break lights appeared in the blackness and started moving toward him. *Shit, they were backing out.*

Trevor spotted a row of dense hedges at the end of the driveway; it was his only place to hide. He crouched down in the bushes and pulled his hood over his head, as if that would make a difference. He felt ridiculous sneaking around and hiding like a child, but it was necessary in a neighborhood like this. Peering through the thick leaves, he watched as the car reversed at a painstakingly slow pace. *C'mon grandma.*

His eyes were focused on the car when he heard a rustling sound in the bushes next to him. He slowly turned his head to find two glowing eyes staring back at him. A high-pitched hissing sound followed, and before he could react, something jumped out at him. On pure instinct, Trevor shielded his face with his arms, falling backwards onto the wet grass. Tiny claws thrashed out at him—the damn thing was attacking him!

It was vicious, squealing and scratching so furiously, it ripped right through his sweatshirt. Trevor could feel the razor-sharp claws cutting into his flesh as he fiercely tried to fling it off. But the animal was in a frenzy, and it took all of his strength to finally push it away. Only seconds had passed, but the damage was done. Warm red blotches of blood were seeping into the sleeve of his right arm. *This was not how it was supposed to go...*

Light-headed and a little dazed, he staggered to his feet. Getting the hell out of there was his only option now. Just as he turned toward the truck, he heard someone approaching from behind. *Shit.* His mind began racing. How would he explain this? *Think Trevor.*

He wouldn't turn around. He would just bolt—he would run to the truck and take off.

"Hey!"

Trevor froze when he heard the voice. As if his feet had a mind of their own, they pivoted one hundred and eighty degrees towards the voice. Out of the shadow of an oak tree, a figure emerged. And it wasn't a grandma; it was a girl. A really cute girl.

In the early morning light, he could see her hair was black and cut short—shorter than his—and her skin was pale. She kind of had the Goth look going, except for the clothes. She was wearing a school uniform, complete with a blazer and one of those little plaid skirts.

"Are you okay?" She cracked a smile, showing a set of perfect teeth. Her eyes moved down to his arm and he tried to cover the shredded sleeve. But the blood was everywhere, and he could see the concern cross her face. He needed to explain himself fast.

"Uh, yeah, I'm fine…" He reached out and offered his left hand. He didn't know what else to do. "I'm Trevor."

She didn't move. Her eyes were still fixated on his bloody arm. He took off his hooded sweatshirt and hurriedly began wrapping it around his arm. "It's not that bad—really. It looks worse than it feels." The truth was it hurt like hell.

Silence hung in the air and Trevor couldn't find any words. He could feel the heat from his wounded arm rising up to his face.

Thankfully, she broke the silence, "Well what happened? I heard a screeching noise. It sounded like a wild animal or something."

Trevor made a feeble attempt at a smile. "Actually it was a wild animal. I think it was a raccoon." He needed to get out of there, but he found himself unable to move.

Goth girl was looking him up and down as if she was trying to decide something. He didn't know what she was thinking, but her gaze was making him uneasy. Would she call the police on him for trespassing?

He wasn't going to take his chances. He was about to turn and leave for a second time, when she suddenly stepped forward. "That looks really bad. Why don't you come in the house and I'll get you a bandage or something."

"Uh…" *Jesus, say something!*

She stepped forward again until she was only inches away. Pulling back a piece of the shredded sleeve, she examined his arm, "I think you really need to get this cleaned up."

She was so close, he could see the sprinkle of freckles on her nose. She had bright blue eyes and pouty lips. Her face was flawless. Trevor felt something stir inside of him.

He thought about her offer for another half a second, "Okay, yeah. Thanks."

For some weird reason, he didn't care about the Honda anymore. He didn't care about his bloodied arm. He didn't even care about getting his ass kicked by Uncle Gary.

All he cared about was following her into that house.

CHAPTER 4

Goth girl turned toward the house and Trevor followed her up the driveway. The closer they got, the more uneasy he began to feel. Her house wasn't just big; it was massive. It had a traditional red brick exterior with enormous stone pillars framing the front entrance. He could count at least eight giant Palladian windows spanning the front of the house. In the center of the front lawn stood a fountain, encircled with more swan statues. Someone obviously liked swans.

She put a key into the enormous front door and pushed it open. The inside of the house was no less impressive. Trevor had never been inside a house close to this size. A large foyer led into a great room with wall-to-wall windows overlooking the lake. He would guess that one room was probably as big as Uncle Gary's entire house. One wall was covered by a vast stone fireplace, flanked by floor-to-ceiling bookshelves. The soaring ceiling was beamed with a rich dark wood that matched the floor.

"Holy shit," was all he could manage to utter. This girl was loaded. Talk about someone from the other side of the tracks.

A huge portrait hung over the mantel—a mom, a dad, and a girl in the middle. It took him a few seconds to realize the girl in the portrait was Goth girl. The face was the same, but the hair was completely different— long and blond. In fact, the whole family looked like they came straight out of a Ralph Lauren advertisement. They all wore big smiles and coordinating plaid outfits. Her mom was an attractive blond and her dad sadly, the same.

Goth girl's voice echoed as she walked away, "I'll be right back."

What the hell am I doing here? Trevor knew coming here was a dumb move, but he couldn't seem to help himself. Maybe he should just turn around and bolt out the front door. Maybe he should say goodbye first…

Before he could decide anything, she appeared from the hall, a box of bandages in her hand and a big smile on her face. Again, he felt the unfamiliar fluttering sensation in his chest. His face felt hot, but it wasn't anxiety, at least the anxiety he was used to. *What was happening to him?* Trevor quickly pointed to the portrait, "Your parents?"

She barely glanced up, "Yep, that's them. One big, happy family." Her voice was dripping with sarcasm.

"Nice place. What do your parents do for a living?"

She sighed, "Well, my dad's some kind of investor. I'm not exactly sure what he does, to tell you the truth. And my mom owns a few salons in the area." She couldn't sound less enthused.

"Wow." It was all he could manage as he looked around.

"Yeah. Wow." One thing became immediately obvious. She didn't like to talk about her parents. He and Goth girl definitely had that in common.

She sat on the couch and smiled at him. "Okay, come over here and let me take a look." She patted the spot next to her.

He walked across the gleaming wood floor and sat down next to her. The couch was more like a loveseat, just big enough for two. Their knees were touching, and as she leaned in closer, he could smell her citrusy perfume.

She pushed up the sleeve on his shirt and Trevor felt himself break out in goose bumps. She gently dabbed at his cuts with a wet cloth. It felt like a thousand bee stings but for some reason, he didn't care one bit.

He tried not to be obvious, but he couldn't stop looking at her face. She really did have pretty eyes. And he noticed she was wearing shiny pink lip gloss. Did she just put that on for him?

He wanted to know more about her—a lot more. *Shit*. He just realized he had never asked her name. "Hey, you never told me your name."

She looked away and began searching through the first aid box. "It's Bea".

26

Not the most common name he had ever heard, "Just B? Is that short for something?"

She began dabbing some clear goo on his cuts. "Okay, well my real name is Barbara, which I hate. I think I may have been named after Barbara Bush, if you can believe it. My dad is a big fan of the whole Bush family."

Oh God no.

"When I was a kid, everyone started calling me Barbie."

At that Trevor had to bite his lip; this was getting pretty funny.

She was blushing, "I know, right. The only name I hate more than Barbara is Barbie."

The more she talked, the more he liked her. "So one day my friend Kate started calling me Bea and it kind of stuck. But to my parents, I am still 'Barbara Eleanor Stewart'. Just my friends call me Bea."

"Okay...so I guess that means were friends?" he asked. He could feel his face get even hotter.

"I guess so." Bea carefully wrapped a mesh bandage around his arm. She would make a great nurse. He definitely liked being her patient. "So Trevor, are you from around here?" she asked.

Something inside him did a somersault when she said his name. His heart was beating so fast! He suddenly couldn't think straight. "Uh, no...I'm from Westwood actually."

She stopped taping the bandage and looked at him, "Really? I've never been there."

No surprise there. Why would someone like her to venture into shitty old Westwood? "It's okay I guess."

"So, I have to ask. What you were doing out here?" She didn't sound accusatory, just curious.

Trevor's mind started racing. This was it. The moment of truth—or the moment of lies—which was it going to be? Before he could say anything, Bea lifted up his bandaged arm and kissed it. "All better," she said grinning.

He didn't want to lie to her. He would tell her the truth...well, most of the truth anyway.

CHAPTER 5

"Darn it!" shouted Lorene.

Bea looked up from her biology homework, "What's wrong?"

"I just sucked up an earring," she said peering into the long vacuum hose. She sat on the ground and opened up the vacuum. The little gold bobble gleamed amidst the dirt and grime in the canister. "Is this yours?" she held it up to Bea.

"Lorene, I don't have pierced ears, remember?"

"Oh, that's right." How could Lorene have forgotten? She was the one who had taken the girl three different times to get them pierced. Except they never got pierced—because every time Bea looked at the piercing gun, she almost fainted. Bea got squeamish that way.

"It must be your mom's." Lorene set it on the table and started up the vacuum again.

Lorene was the Stewart family housekeeper. She came to the house when Bea was six years old and had played the role of mother and friend and everything in-between. Monday through Friday, at six-thirty a.m., she got on the bus at East 220th street in Cleveland. She rode into downtown, and boarded another bus that took her out of the city, along the lakeshore, and into Harbor Village.

Anyone living in the area knew that the west side and the east side of Cleveland were essentially worlds apart. Geographically they were separated by downtown and Lake Erie to the north, but culturally they were separated as well.

After a few trips to the grocery store, Lorene quickly learned there weren't many black folks living in the western suburbs. It wasn't just the fact that she never ran into any. It was also the way white people reacted to her—just slightly surprised to see her. It was very subtle, but enough that she noticed.

She joked with her husband Reggie about it, "I know Harbor Village is only across town, but I swear, it feels like I'm on a different planet."

Lorene and Reggie had been married thirty-two years and it had never been boring. He was an architect for a local construction firm and she had always stayed home with the kids. When the kids were in high school, she wanted to make some extra money. Retirement wasn't far off for Reggie and they eventually wanted to travel more, see the world. That's when she took the housekeeping job at the Stewarts.

The truth was they had saved enough money to buy a house in the more upscale suburbs, but they were comfortable where they were. They didn't want to be labeled as the 'black family' that moved in. Reggie had always said that was part of the problem. People want to stay where they're comfortable.

Maybe that's why she had stayed with the Stewarts for eleven years. Lorene was comfortable there. That, and the fact that she couldn't even think about leaving Bea alone in that crazy house.

"Lorene, I've got to tell you something!" Bea suddenly blurted out.

Her cheeks were flushed and she was grinning from ear to ear. The girl was a stunner, and the older she got, the more beautiful she became. Thankfully, she also had a good head on her shoulders.

At every chance she got, Lorene had tried to instill positive values in her. Lord knows she didn't get any guidance from her parents. Lorene had always emphasized the importance of judging people based on what's inside, and not their outside appearance.

This life lesson may have been what spurred Bea's dramatic decision last summer to cut off all her hair. And to top it off, she dyed her naturally blond hair, jet black. Lord, did that make Mrs. Stewart furious.

Lorene put the vacuum hose down and sat at the table. "Sounds serious. What is it?"

The girl was beaming, "I met a boy!"

This was news. "Really? A boy?" Bea never talked about boys.

"Yeah, and Lorene he is so nice. His name is Trevor." She was almost giddy. "He's really cute."

Lorene was happy for her and wanted to hear more. "Well, tell me everything. Where'd you meet him? I know it wasn't at school."

Bea went to a private all-girls high school. She was in the end of her junior year and hated it. Well maybe hate was too strong a word, but she definitely wouldn't be there if she had any choice in the matter. She despised the uniforms and complained about how most of the girls were snobs. "It isn't the real world" she would say. Lorene had news for her. This bubble of rich suburbia wasn't the real world either. Bea was a good girl but she was still a little naïve.

"That's the kind of weird thing. I met him here. Well, actually in the front yard…down by the street," Bea was suddenly stammering.

Lorene raised one eyebrow. This was curious indeed.

"Don't look at me like that!"

Lorene tried to put on her best poker face, "Go on."

"Well, he's really nice. Probably around my age. I met him this morning before school. I heard this strange noise when I was pulling out of the driveway… See, he got scratched really badly by a raccoon and I…"

"What?" Lorene interrupted. "Did you say a raccoon?"

"Yeah," Bea was avoiding her eyes, "And so I had to help him, you know, clean it up and stuff."

Lorene was afraid to ask the next question, "So, you let him into the house?"

Bea looked at Lorene with her 'Please don't be mad at me' face, "Well I needed to get him some bandages. He was really hurt."

Lorene shook her head. She thought she had taught the girl to be more careful. "So, what was he doing? Walking to school or something?"

"Not exactly…" A sheepish smile was forming on Bea's face. "He's not from around here."

Lorene began picking at her cuticles. It was a bad habit that she only resorted to when getting exceptionally nervous. "Okay, where's he from?"

"I'm not sure. He might've said Westwood."

Westwood was a twenty minute drive. "So what was he doing *here*?"

Bea's silly grin still hadn't left her face. Lorene was exasperated. "Would you please tell me? As much as I love a little suspense, I've got to get dinner started."

Bea's voice got quiet and she looked at the ground, "He was… garbage-picking."

Lorene sat back in her chair, not saying what she was thinking. *Oh this was rich. This was rich indeed.*

CHAPTER 6

After school Trevor headed over to his sanctuary in the backyard. He called it the Box. To anyone on the outside it just looked like a run-down garage. To him it was a haven, a place where he could do what he loved. It was an escape from all of the chaos in his world.

But today it was going to be hard to concentrate on work. He couldn't stop thinking about this morning, about her. He had told Bea pretty much everything. He told her why he was at her house—he told her about the lawnmower and how he wanted to garbage-pick it. She could've been a snob about it, or at the very least laughed at him, but she didn't. In fact, she really didn't seem to care why he was there. She listened to him and didn't judge him, which was pretty cool.

He wasn't an expert at reading girls, but he got a feeling Bea really liked him. Trevor had never had a girlfriend before. Unlike most seventeen year olds, girls weren't the center of his universe.

School wasn't either. He didn't play sports, and he wasn't in band. He didn't join chess club, or pep club, or any other asshole club. He ate alone in the cafeteria and read. Kids pretty much left him alone, and he was sure the term 'freak' was used a lot behind his back.

Some might feel sorry for him, but the truth was, he liked it that way. He went to school and did the bare minimum. His focus was, and always had been, on things outside of school.

Before Trevor left Bea's house, he got her phone number and asked if he could call her sometime. Her exact response was, "Anytime." At school, it was all he could think about.

He got lucky with Uncle Gary's truck too. When he came back from Bea's house, the fat-ass was still asleep. On his way to take another shower, Trevor had peeked into his bedroom only to find Uncle Gary spread eagle on the bed, fully dressed and snoring like a dying animal. A strong whiff of whiskey mixed with cigarettes hit Trevor in the face. It must've been a rough night.

But lately it seemed like every night was a rough one for Uncle Gary. He pretty much stuck to the same routine since Trevor had moved in. Go to the shop, go to the Barley Tavern, go home and pass out. Over the last year, it seemed to be getting worse. Now he was sleeping past eight and having one of his lackeys open up the shop for him.

Uncle Gary was the proud owner of McNulty Mechanics, a small garage shop that dabbled in fixing everything from cars to lawnmowers. They also sold a lot of junk on the side. His uncle had inherited it from Trevor's grandfather, Sean McNulty, twenty years ago.

According to Mr.T, it had been a very respectable business at one time. But then Grandpa McNulty started drinking away his profits and things went downhill quick. When Uncle Gary took over, the shop was just about to go under. He was only around twenty back then, just a little older than Trevor was now.

And Trevor had to give him credit. Uncle Gary managed to save the shop with some creative business ideas. They might be ethically appalling, but financially they were genius. He knew how to scam people and it didn't bother his conscience one bit.

As soon as Trevor stepped foot into his uncle's house, he was lectured on the world according to Gary. A kid like Trevor was only going to get ahead in this world by screwing people over—simple as that. "Honesty won't get you anywhere kid. Being nice won't either. I mean you're always nice to a customer's face, but you aren't nice to their wallet. You understand?"

Trevor just nodded his head and thought to himself, *how can I be related to this idiot?*

The next thing Uncle Gary enlightened him with, was one of his secrets to keeping costs down—garbage-picking. "There is nothing more profitable than selling something you got for free," he would say.

And that's where Trevor really came in handy. If he wanted to live in his house, he had to live by Uncle Gary's rules and earn his keep.

Garbage-picking was like going to one of those early bird specials at Kmart. The key to getting the good stuff was getting out there early—but not too early, or the merchandise wouldn't be ready.

Uncle Gary would say he was too old to be getting up at the crack of dawn. Trevor would say he was too hung over. Regardless, now it would be Trevor's job. In return, he got the privilege of living with one of the biggest assholes on the planet.

But at least Uncle Gary had introduced him to garbage-picking. It may sound strange to some, but this new chore had become a passion to Trevor, a much needed distraction. Of course it could be embarrassing when someone caught him picking through their trash, but he found most people didn't mind at all. In fact, Trevor figured they probably thought of it as an act of charity on their part.

An adrenaline rush always kicked in when he set out early in the morning. Not knowing what he would find was the thrill. It was amazing what some people would throw away: perfectly good furniture, like dressers that just needed new knobs; appliances with blown fuses; toys that kids had simply outgrown. So many things just needed a little work to be useful again. And, if it wasn't for garbage-picking, he never would've gone out to Harbor Village, and he never would've met Bea.

Uncle Gary would never know he went to forbidden territory this morning. He would also never know that he missed out on a Honda HRX. The mower had been just out of reach, on the other side of the tree lawn, the whole time. But by the time he had left Bea's house, it was long gone.

Any other time Trevor would've kicked himself over being so stupid. Those chances didn't come around very often. But neither did the chance to meet a cool girl. No, he couldn't seem to get pissed at anything today, not even himself. Today was a great day. Today was the day he met Bea.

CHAPTER 7

Bea and Lorene sat at the kitchen table finishing their shrimp stir-fry when the side door opened and Evelyn Stewart walked in.

"Hi ladies!" She got an Evian bottle out of the refrigerator. Her blond hair was pulled back in a butterfly clip, her face flushed, but her make-up still perfect. "What a day! God, I'm exhausted." She took a long drink of her water.

Lorene had to give Mrs. Stewart credit for her hard work ethic. Of course, having the money to start up her salons was easy to get, but making them into a successful chain was anything but easy. Although Mrs. Stewart didn't need the money, Lorene figured the woman had to be making a fortune. While dusting in the office last week, Lorene found some of her salon pamphlets and had to take a peek. Eighty-five dollars for a pedicure!

Lorene just didn't understand why women would pay that kind of money to get their toes painted.

"Any packages arrive today?" Mrs. Stewart asked. She was always ordering something from the internet, and packages arrived daily.

"No I didn't see any today," said Lorene. She made a point to check the front porch every day. She could never hear the UPS truck from inside that mammoth house.

"Okay." Mrs. Stewart glanced over at Bea, "So how was your day Barbara?"

Bea was moving a shrimp around the plate with her fork. She shrugged, "It was fine. Same old stuff." Lorene could see the agitation on Bea's face. She despised being called Barbara.

Mrs. Stewart was studying Bea. "Anything going on I should know about?"

Bea glanced up at her mother. "No, nothing new and exciting to report. Oh, I did forget one thing. I get to represent my school at the regional environmental fair."

"That's great honey." Mrs. Stewart walked over and gave her a quick hug. Bea sat motionless.

No mention of the boy. That didn't surprise Lorene. The relationship between Bea and her mother was amicable, but not close like some mothers and daughters were. Bea had definitely paid the price for her mother's success. For most of Bea's childhood, Mrs. Stewart just wasn't there. It wasn't unusual for Bea and her mother to speak via cell phone only—sometimes for days at a time.

And because Bea was an only child, it made things even lonelier. Many days, Lorene found herself staying at the Stewarts later than was required, simply to keep the poor girl company.

"Well, I've got an early meeting with the staff before we open tomorrow. We're introducing a new product line. It's very exciting." Mrs. Stewart had been eyeing the stir-fry since she walked in, "How's the dinner?"

"It's delicious. There's plenty here," said Bea.

"No thanks Hon," she smiled. "I ate at the salon."

Under the table, Bea nudged Lorene with her knee.

"Well, goodnight girls," she said as she started up the staircase. "Oh, and Lorene, before you leave, could you find my Marc Jacobs sweater? The red cashmere one? Thanks." Mrs. Stewart waved over her shoulder and jogged up the stairs.

Bea got up and walked over to the fridge. She took out the chocolate cheesecake Lorene had made for dessert. "Do you want a piece?" she asked, cutting a generous slice for herself.

Lorene took her plate to the sink. "No thanks. I think I'll go look for that sweater before I leave."

"Screw the sweater," Bea muttered from behind. "I think she'll survive without it."

Lorene turned to find Bea sticking a big chunk of cheesecake into her mouth. She wasn't quite sure how to respond to this one. Bea had issues with her mother; there was no doubt about it. But Lorene felt it was best to approach the subject cautiously. Even though she didn't understand Mrs. Stewart's priorities, it was

41

important to stay neutral. Painting Bea's mother in a bad light wouldn't help anything. "Okay, what's this about?"

Bea's mouth was puffed out with cheesecake, but it didn't stop her. "Do you notice how she doesn't eat anything? I mean it's ridiculous! I'm a size six and I look like a cow next to her. She's obsessed with being thin."

"You know what Bea, I think she's just stressed out. She works very hard and it's not easy dealing with those persnickety women all day."

This behavior from Bea was something knew. She never seemed to care much about anything her mom was doing, let alone how much she was eating. Was this jealousy? Lorene didn't think so. Mrs. Stewart was a beautiful woman, but so was Bea. The girl was probably just worried about her mother, and unfortunately, she had good reason to be.

Mrs. Stewart had lost a lot of weight. Lorene thought the weight loss probably had to do with the stress of her job, or the fact that she was turning the big four-0 soon. Or, it could be because Mrs. Stewart was insecure and didn't think she looked good enough for that jackass she was married to.

Bea's father, Bill Stewart, was intolerable to Lorene. He was a prominent business man in Cleveland and was on the board of directors for several companies. He was never home, and fortunately, she only ran into him on rare occasions.

Lord, the man was full of himself. Yes, he was good-looking if you were into the tall, light and handsome. But even someone who looked like Robert Redford—and probably had as much money as him—didn't impress Lorene. Unless he had a strong character, all of the other traits meant nothing. The man acted so self-important, it was almost unbearable to be in the same room with him.

The Stewarts obviously didn't have the time to do their own shopping, so Lorene bought everything: the groceries, the clothes, even the toiletries. Early on in her employment, Mr. Stewart presented her with a computerized list of what he needed on a weekly and monthly basis. The man used more products than any woman Lorene had ever known. Anti-wrinkle lotion, eye-firming serum, exfoliating scrub, clay mask, night-time cream, day-time cream…and this was all just for his face!

All of these items were purchased at the cosmetics counter at Sak's. No Wal-Mart products in his bathroom. When she bought him the Armani aftershave lotion in original formula instead of the sensitive skin formula, he acted like she had handed him a bottle of piss water.

"Hello? Lorene?" Bea interrupted her thoughts. "Don't you think so?"

"Sorry Hon. Think what?"

Bea shoveled another huge forkful of cheesecake into her mouth, "That she's starting to look anorexic."

All Lorene could do was shrug, "I do think she's a little too thin." But weight loss didn't seem to be Mrs. Stewart's only problem. Lorene didn't tell Bea, but Mrs. Stewart had started closet-drinking.

Over the last few months, Lorene had found several empty bottles of Absolut under the bathroom sink. Absolut vodka was Mrs. Stewart's drink of choice—but usually with cranberry and a lime—not straight out of the bottle.

But, if anyone could drive a person to drink, it was Bill Stewart. Lord knows if Lorene had been married to that horse's ass, she would've been in the crazy house a long time ago.

***

Lorene got off the bus and started walking home. Another week was done and it had been an eventful one. Bea's news about the boy was a surprise. She wasn't sure what was going to come of it, but it would be interesting when Mr. and Mrs. Stewart found out. Lorene had a feeling that a garbage picker from Westwood would not be the Stewart's first choice of an ideal boyfriend for their only daughter.

She opened the front door of her colonial on Revere Road. Although she was technically in Cleveland city limits, she lived in one of the nicer areas on the East side. They were close to two prominent universities as well as the museums and the orchestra hall.

She hoped Reggie was home. She needed to let off some steam and he was a good sounding board. He always listened and acted interested, even when she knew he wasn't. "Hey honey!" She hung her jacket on a hook by the door and went into the kitchen. She always brought home the leftovers for Reggie. It was close to eight o'clock, but he didn't mind a late dinner.

"I'm on the porch!" Reggie yelled from the back of the house.

Lorene joined Reggie on the porch, sitting on a wicker chair and putting her feet up on the ottoman. "What a week."

Reggie was hunched over his work table. "Yeah? What's happening over in rich-man's land?" he asked, paintbrush in hand.

Reggie collected model trains. In the evenings he would spend hours on the three-season porch working on his hobby. In the corner of the porch, sat a large display table with a replica countryside on top. A myriad of railroad tracks crossed over mountains and through tunnels. All of his train cars were Lionel, and they all were made prior to 1960. Depending on their condition, he could spend days on one car, sometimes even months.

"Oh, I'm just a little worried about Bea, that's all."

"Okay…" He dipped his paintbrush into some red paint. "Tell me about it."

"You're going to think I'm over-reacting, but I just have a really bad feeling about something. See, she met this boy, and she was so excited about it. I can tell she really likes him."

"Well that doesn't sound so bad. She's like seventeen isn't she? This is the time she's going to start dating and all that."

Lorene got up and walked back into the kitchen. "I know. But let me tell you how they met. You'll love this." She took out a frying pan to warm up the shrimp stir-fry. "She's going to school in the morning, pulling out the driveway, and she sees this kid getting up off the ground." She peeked around the corner into the porch. "Are you listening to me?"

Reggie stopped painting, "Yes, I heard you Lorene."

"Well, get this. Bea sees that his arm is bleeding badly. Blood all over the kid's sweatshirt. Apparently, he had been attacked by a raccoon. Can you believe that?"

Reggie looked up, a big smile on his face, "Are you kidding me?"

"I swear," she put her hands up in the air. "And guess why he got attacked by that raccoon?"

"I know you're going to tell me," Reggie chuckled.

"He was hiding in some bushes at the end of the Stewart's driveway. And you may ask, 'Why was he hiding in the bushes Lorene?' And I would tell you, because he was garbage-picking!"

Reggie shook his head, "Oh no."

Lorene went on, "I know! Can you just see Bill Stewart's face? 'Hey daddy, I'd like you to meet my new boyfriend. I met him while he was picking through our garbage.' Oh, it's just too much Reggie."

"Well you know what they say..."

"To each his own," Lorene replied. "To each his own."

CHAPTER 8

Today was Saturday and that meant Trevor could spend the whole day in the Box. He got a shower and then headed downstairs. Uncle Gary was sitting at the kitchen table drinking his coffee, probably nursing another hangover. "Hey, you pick up anything good lately?" he asked.

Trevor took a can of pop out of the fridge. "Uh, not really…but Frank told me about this house where this rich lady lived. She had to move into a nursing home and I guess they're cleaning out her house. Getting rid of good stuff every week. It's in Lowell and I think trash day is Tuesday."

"Shit, Frank doesn't know his ass from a hole in the ground. You better get on it. It's been a while since you brought me anything worth a damn."

Uncle Gary didn't like Frank, probably because Frank was a nice guy with a wife and a family. Trevor met Frank two years ago when he was out scouting the streets. He drove past a kid's bike that looked salvageable, but by the time he turned around and parked the pickup, the garbage truck was there. One of the garbage men was getting ready to throw it in the truck when Trevor yelled from across the street, "Hey! Wait!"

Holding the bike up in a mid-throw stance, the garbage man halted and waited for him to cross. The man looked at him curiously, "Can I help you kid?"

Trevor knew he sounded pathetic but he didn't care. He wanted that bike. "Don't throw it away. Can I have it?"

The man looked at the bike's cracked frame, "You sure you want it?"

"Yeah, I'm sure." The bike did look like a piece of crap, but Trevor was convinced he could fix it.

The garbage man shrugged his shoulders and tossed the bike to him, "Suit yourself."

As Trevor turned to leave, a thought came to him. "Hey! Is this your route every Wednesday, at the same time?"

"Yeah pretty much. Why?"

Feeling like he had to prove something, Trevor said loudly, "Okay. I'll be here next week with this bike, and it will look brand new!"

"Yeah, whatever kid." The garbage man was shaking his head as he jumped on the back of the truck. "Got to go!"

Another idea immediately popped into Trevor's head. It might be beneficial to have a friend in the garbage business. Maybe he could get an inside track to the good stuff. Maybe, they could even make some kind of deal. "Hey! What's your name?" he yelled after the man.

"Frank!" the man yelled back as the truck drove away.

Trevor waved, "See you next week Frank!"

And it was right there, standing among a slew of empty garbage cans, where Trevor first had the idea about the Box. He could turn that old garage into a workshop. He could fix more than just appliances, and motors, and all the other junk Uncle Gary wanted. He could fix things like toys and furniture. He had a broken bike, a deadline, and most important, he had a purpose.

"Piss-ant, did you hear me?" Uncle Gary broke up his thoughts. "I said you need to do some laundry today. Don't go hiding in that garage all day."

The only thing Trevor hated more than cleaning up after that pig—which was disgusting enough—was doing his laundry. He would not wish that job on his worst enemy. In order to survive it, he had learned the art of breathing through the mouth perfectly.

"Yeah okay, I'll get to it today," and Trevor was out the back door.

When he got in the Box he immediately felt better. *Home*. He walked over to his work station and started setting up the table saw. Before he knew it, his thoughts turned to Bea. It had only been one day, but he really wanted to see her again. He couldn't decide if he should call her now or wait until tonight. Would he seem too desperate? He decided to text her instead; it was easier.

Hey, what's up Barbara?

It was only a few seconds and then he heard the 'ding-dong' alerting him of a new text message. *Not much, u?*

Just working in the Box, he typed.

Sounds fun. I'd luv 2 c it

Trevor panicked. Bea wanted to come to his house. She already knew he lived in Westwood with his white-trash uncle. He had told her the truth about that. Sooner or later, if things went the way he hoped, she would have to see where he lived.

Screw it. *Do you want to come over?* He hit 'send' and held his breath.

His phone lit up immediately. *What's your address? B there in 20*

After giving her the address, he ran back into the house. Thankfully, Uncle Gary left in his truck, which probably meant he would be at the bar all day. Trevor brushed his teeth again and checked out his face in the mirror. No zits. He only got zits occasionally, and luckily none today. He had shaved this morning and no razor burn either—double bonus. His hair was probably a little long, but there was nothing he could do about that now. He reapplied his deodorant and checked his grey sweatshirt for stains—this was one of the few decent shirts he owned.

He ran back to the Box and tried to stay busy, but it was pretty much impossible. Ten minutes later he heard a car pull up into the gravel driveway. He was nervous as hell. His heart was racing and he had to keep wiping his sweaty hands on his jeans.

He could only imagine what Bea was thinking. Westwood must be like a foreign country to her. She was probably afraid to get out of the car.

Peeking out the side window, he could see Bea walking into the backyard. She was wearing jeans and a short white sweater. Unlike the bulky school uniform, this outfit showed off all of her curves. His heart lurched in his chest—what was happening to him?

He swallowed hard, opened the door and walked out. "Hey, did you find it okay?" He tried to sound casual.

She was about to answer him when Jip ran to her at full speed and began jumping up.

"Jip! Get down! Jip…down!" he yelled at the dog.

Bea didn't seem to mind. She bent down and started petting Jip on the head. "Oh he's so cute…he's adorable. I always wanted a dog, but my parents would never allow it." Jip immediately rolled over onto his back hoping for a belly-scratch. Thank God for Jip; he totally broke the ice.

"That name's kind of different. Where'd you get the name Jip?" she asked.

He could feel his face flushing, "Well, it's kind of dumb…"

She looked up at him smiling, "So, I want to hear it."

"Okay." He noticed big dimples in her cheeks. "You sure?"

She nodded again showing her perfect white smile.

"Okay. Here goes. Well, Abraham Lincoln had a dog named Jip. The story is that soldiers found him in confederate territory and he was almost frozen to death. The soldiers gave the dog to the president." Trevor kneeled down and started scratching Jip behind the ears. "And Mr.T found this guy in his backyard almost frozen to death, so I thought the name fit." *God, he sounded lame.*

"I think it definitely fits. Who's Mr.T?" she asked.

Trevor must not have mentioned his seventy year old best friend, "Oh, that's Mr.Tyminski. He lives next door. We hang out a lot. He's a real good guy." Then he added, "And he's like seventy."

"Really?" He could hear the surprise in her voice.

He avoided her eyes, "I know it seems weird, but he's really cool. Kind of like a grandpa I never had. You'd like him."

When he finally had the courage to look at her, she seemed to be studying him. "How do you know this stuff? I mean, like about Abraham Lincoln's dog?"

Trevor shrugged his shoulders, "I don't know. I read a lot?"

"Well, do I get to see inside the Box?" she asked, looking over his shoulder at the garage. No one other than Mr.T had ever set foot inside the Box.

"Yeah come on in," he said as he got up. Holding out his hand, he helped her to her feet. He led her to the Box, not letting go of her hand.

When Trevor opened the door, he could hear Bea suck in her breath. He caught a sideways glance at her face. She was holding her hand up over her mouth and her eyes were wide, "Holy crap!"

She was definitely surprised.

CHAPTER 9

Tom didn't recognize the car in the driveway or the girl that wandered into the Box with Trevor. So the kid had finally met a friend his own age, and a pretty girl at that. He hoped this was a sign of more good things to come. The kid needed to start opening up to people, preferably people not on social security. Maybe the sessions with Dr. Fisher were making a difference.

When Trevor first gave Tom a tour of the Box and showed him all of the projects he was working on, Tom was truly impressed. Here was a kid who had been to hell and back, and he still wanted to do something productive with his time.

One day Trevor had asked him for help with an air-conditioning unit. After researching on the internet, the kid still couldn't figure out which fuse to replace. Spending over forty years as an electrician, Tom knew everything there was to know about fuses, and they fixed it together. Things were going so well, Tom thought it was a good time to bring up an idea he had been tossing around in his mind for a while. He asked Trevor if he had ever thought about going to a doctor.

"What do you mean? I'm perfectly healthy. I think you should worry about your own old ass." The kid didn't understand that Tom was suggesting a therapist.

"No, I mean a doctor that can help with your problems."

When the realization hit, Trevor got ticked off. "What, you think I need a shrink? You think I'm crazy?"

Tom held up his hands, "No, no…nothing like that. It's just sometimes it's good to talk to someone about things. Someone objective, someone that doesn't judge you. You just get some things off your chest you know. I've been to one before. It helps."

"Well no thanks Mr.T," he said. "Not interested."

"Okay," Tom didn't want to give up. "But you like making deals right? You have a pretty good deal with that garbage man, what's his name, Frank?"

"Yeah, what about it?"

Tom chose his words carefully. "Well I was thinking. You could really use some new tools and stuff to fix up the place. And I would be willing to help you buy that stuff if you do something for me."

"What? Like go to a shrink? What does that do for you Mr.T? Deals go both ways. Frank gives me tips—I give him something I fixed up. That's how it works."

Trevor started looking through his screwdriver drawer. "Did you see the tiny Phillips head screwdriver?" He wouldn't look Tom in the eye. "Besides, I'm sure you just have tons of money to be throwing around. Tools aren't cheap."

"Here." The screwdriver was sitting on the work table, right under the kid's nose. "I have enough money kid. What do I spend it on anyway—heating bills and TV dinners? I have some extra."

Tom thought of Trevor like his own grandson. The kid was family to him, and Tom worried about him. After everything he had been through, what the kid needed most was professional help. There was too much he was hiding under the surface, and if he didn't talk to someone about it, who knows what would happen.

Trevor began twisting the screwdriver faster, still avoiding Tom's eyes. "Can there be some conditions?"

Tom laughed under a sigh of relief, "Absolutely. Name them."

The kid insisted on picking his own doctor. Tom thought he could probably arrange that without a problem. He also insisted everything that happened behind closed doors stayed there—he didn't want a million questions. Of course Tom respected that.

Then Tom laid out his one and only condition. Trevor had to go to the Beaumont Center because that was the best. "When you get done with a session, you get a Home Depot gift card," he told the kid.

"How much?" Trevor asked immediately.

"Now you sound like a teenager!" Tom laughed. "Don't worry kid. You won't be disappointed."

And the kid hadn't been. Trevor worked his butt off with every penny he got, and turned the Box into a workshop any man would envy.

Tom grabbed his spring jacket and headed out the door. The kid wasn't the only one with a hot date today. He had called Sorak's diner to ask Carol if she would be working this afternoon. She sounded happy to hear from him. He was actually a little excited to see her—and to get those noodles.

***

Trevor had to admit, from the outside the Box looked like nothing more than a run-down garage. He wanted it that way; he didn't need his uncle snooping around. But thanks to Mr.T, the inside had been completely gutted and renovated. And it was spotless.

Steel-topped cabinets lined one wall. On top of the cabinets were shelves that held clear plastic containers. They were filled with every type of hardware imaginable and everything was neatly labeled. Paint cans were packed under the cabinets in color-coordinated sections.

Along a second wall was a large workstation with overhead pendant lights. Mr.T had to help him with the wiring on those. The station had saws, drills, and various other tools, all hung in orderly rows on the pegboard behind it.

The third wall, directly across from them, was what Trevor was most proud of. The Wall of Garbage. The entire wall was covered in photographs from floor to ceiling. It looked like a giant piece of abstract art. It was filled with hundreds of before-and-after shots of everything Trevor had ever garbage-picked and fixed up. A stove, a wheelbarrow, a clock, a stroller…something filled every conceivable space on the wall. All of the items looked like junk in the 'before' and brand new in the 'after'.

"You did all this?" Bea's eyes were riveted to the wall, her voice quiet.

Trevor felt his face flushing, again. "Yeah, this is what I was telling you about. It all came out of the garbage-picking."

She hurried over to the wall. "This is incredible! So do you sell all this stuff?"

He joined her at the wall and caught a glimpse of the bike he had given Frank. "Actually, I don't sell it. I have to give a lot of it to my uncle. He was the one who kind of made me go garbage-picking in the first place. He has a mechanics shop in town—don't ask."

He paused, feeling a little embarrassed, although he wasn't sure why, "And the rest I usually give away to people."

Bea looked at him like he was crazy, "What? You give it away? Like donate it?"

He laughed, "Yeah. I'm on a first name basis with the volunteers at the Goodwill and Salvation Army stores."

"Seriously?" She was quiet for a minute, studying the wall. "You do realize you could get some serious money for this stuff. You know, sell it on EBay or something."

Trevor shrugged his shoulders. He had really never considered selling any of it. "Yeah, probably." He walked over to the workstation and fiddled with some drill bits. "I guess giving it away just...feels right, you know?"

He knew that probably sounded lame but it was the truth. He would never forget the look on Frank's face when he brought that bike back to him. Trevor worked his ass off on that thing. It looked brand new—painted fire engine red with yellow flame decals on the frame. As it turns out, Frank had an eleven-year old son with an upcoming birthday. From then on, Frank was all too happy to show his appreciation. He became Trevor's inside guy to the best stuff on the garbage routes.

"Come over here," Trevor reached out and grabbed her hand again. He led her over to the workbench. Sitting under the lights was one of his current projects, an old wooden rocking horse. "I actually found this at a garage sale on my way home from school—they only wanted a dollar for it."

"Awe, it's adorable," she ran her hand over the unfinished wood.

"I've been sanding it. Then I just need to paint it and get a new rope for the reigns. I'm taking it to the Haven House. They call it a crisis nursery. It's one of those places where kids go before they're placed in foster care."

She looked up at him. They were so close, he could smell her citrusy perfume again. "Wow. Isn't it sad seeing all those kids?"

"You'd be surprised. The kids there are amazing. Most of them have experienced some pretty awful things, but you wouldn't know it. I've only been there twice so far, but I definitely plan on going again."

The Haven House was affiliated with the same hospital as the Crazy Kids Center. After Trevor's first session with Dr. Fisher, he noticed bright green flyers hanging all over the walls in the lobby. They were announcing a fundraiser to benefit the Haven House, which it turns out, was located on the outskirts of Westwood. It was only a few minutes from his house by bike. That's when he had the idea of fixing up the toys.

"This is really amazing Trevor."

Hearing the admiration in her voice made him excited, but nervous at the same time. He was letting her into a part of his world that only Mr.T had seen. Still, he couldn't stop talking, "The best was when I delivered the toys. The kids came running up to me like I was Santa Claus. It was awesome, really."

God, he hoped he didn't sound like an egomaniac. He wasn't trying to come off as some kind of saint. It was just so nice to share it all with her.

"How did you learn to fix all this stuff? I mean, I could never learn to do all this."

"Yes you could. You would be surprised how much you can learn from the internet. Another one of my favorite places is the library because they have free internet access. I spend a lot of time there."

Then he added, "And of course Mr.T helps me a lot. He used to be an electrician so he's taught me a ton."

"Is he the one who bought you all the tools and stuff?" she asked. "I mean you said your uncle was pretty much a jerk, so I was just curious."

"Yeah, Mr.T's a pretty cool guy."

"Wow, he just gives it to you?"

Trevor had no intention of telling Bea about his deal with Mr.T yet. He just wasn't ready to go into the whole Crazy Kids Center and his sessions with Dr. Fisher. Hell no. "Well I help him around his house a lot." He stopped there and looked her in the eyes. "What is this? Twenty questions?"

She looked embarrassed and Trevor immediately followed with, "Kidding… I like the questions, really." He had no clue how to act around girls.

"I'm sorry. I think it's awesome—all of it. You know, I would really like to go with you next time you go to Haven House."

Trevor turned to her, but she immediately looked down at the floor. He put his arms around her waist and pulled her closer to him. He felt her arms wrap around his back. Good sign. He was being pretty forward, but they were alone, and he really wanted to kiss her. This was the perfect opportunity.

Trevor had been thinking about kissing Bea since they first met. Sadly, although he was seventeen, he had never come close to kissing a girl. Mr.T was always asking if he had met any girls or gone out on any dates. Honestly, he just never had any interest in girls, until now. God, he hoped he didn't screw it up.

He started to lean down, closer, closer…

"You know what—" she abruptly pulled away from him and looked away. "I better get going." And just like that, she turned around and dashed out the door.

Trevor stood there dumbfounded. What in the hell just happened?

CHAPTER 10

Lorene was doing her thing in the kitchen. She truly loved cooking. On the center island sat a cutting board and a colander full of fresh vegetables. She was stuffing some pasta shells with spinach and ricotta cheese. Bea walked in from school and dropped into a kitchen chair.

"Hey Bea, how was school?"

"It was okay." She sounded a little down. "What's for dinner? I'm starving."

"Oh just some stuffed shells with salad."

"Sounds good." Bea started digging through her bag for her homework.

Lorene began chopping the vegetables for the salad. "So, did you talk to that boy over the weekend? The one you were telling me about—what's his name—Trevor?"

"Yeah, I actually went over to visit him on Saturday. He's really sweet."

Lorene remembered Bea had mentioned he was from Westwood. "So, does he go to school in Westwood? That's where he's from, right?"

"Yeah. He goes to Westwood High. He's a junior." The girl didn't seem to be in the mood to talk.

Just then Lorene dropped the salad spoons and ran over to the range. "Oh shoot! I forgot to put on the oven."

"Trevor told me he is a vegetarian you know. Do you think that's weird?"

This did surprise Lorene. "Really? You don't see many teenage boys turning vegetarian. But I wouldn't say it's weird—more like unique."

Lorene went back to tossing the salad. "So what are his plans for after high school?"

"I'm not sure. We didn't really talk about that." Bea didn't like the question. Lorene could hear it in her tone.

Lorene placed the bread dough in a loaf pan. She couldn't help herself. Just one more question, "Do you think—?"

Before she could finish, Bea was shouting, "What the hell is this Lorene? An inquisition? Like I said, we didn't talk about it. And what if he doesn't want to go to college? What if he just wants to be an artist, or a plumber, or a fireman, or whatever. Does it really matter?"

Lorene had pushed too far. "Honey, I'm sorry. I was just curious, that's all. Sometimes I just don't know when to shut up."

Bea wouldn't look her in the eyes. She slumped down in her chair, a pitiful frown on her face. "Sorry. I just feel kind of stressed out lately. On Saturday, I kind of just ran out on him."

Uh oh. "You did? Did something upset you?"

Bea sighed, "Not really. I mean, he didn't do anything. I guess I just freaked out, you know. Everything was a little overwhelming."

An idea popped into Lorene's head, "You know what? Why don't you call Trevor up and ask him over for dinner? This is a completely vegetarian meal. Your mom won't be home until late tonight. And, I'd really like to meet him."

Bea's eyes lit up. "Really? That would be awesome. I just hope he's not mad about the way I left on Saturday. Talk about embarrassing." In seconds she was digging in her bag for her cell phone. "Oh well, I guess I'll just have to call him up and see. I know you're really going to like him Lorene."

Lorene could hear her leaving a message, sounding very casual. Bea must really like this boy, and Lorene was happy for her. She truly hoped she would get to meet him tonight.

***

On his way home from school, Trevor checked his phone. He had a voicemail waiting from Bea. She invited him over for dinner, saying her parents wouldn't be around and they'd have the place to themselves.

He was surprised. After Bea left on Saturday, he thought she wanted nothing more to do with him. And, dinner was a tempting offer, but the whole situation was starting to stress him out. As much as he liked Bea, he wasn't used to the drama. I mean, she walks out right when he was about to kiss her? He would never understand girls.

But the bigger problem was that Bea was living in another world. She hadn't asked him about the rest of his family yet. She didn't even ask why he was living with his uncle. What would she think when she found out the truth? How could she ever understand? And shit, what would her super rich parents think?

Trevor didn't want to deal with it now. He just wanted to work in his Box and clear his head. He would just send her a text and say he couldn't make it.

He typed into his phone: *Hey, I'm really tired and not feeling up 2 dinner 2nite. Maybe another time? Thx 4 the offer.* At least it was honest.

A couple of minutes later he got a response. *That's fine.* She was pissed.

He texted back, *I would like to c u. Just tired 2nite*
Ok I understand. Sorry about the way I left Saturday.

Now the guilt started settling in. He imagined her sitting there with a pouty look on her face and suddenly he had an overwhelming urge to see her. Did he really want to do this? Screw it.

I am pretty hungry. ☺ Be there in 20?

Just as he was sending the text, Trevor realized he would have to ride his bike there. Uncle Gary wouldn't be back for hours. Harbor Village was about twenty minutes by car, so who knew how long it would take on a bike…unless.

Trevor ran over to Mr.T's.

CHAPTER 11

The damn mail was wet again. That was it—he was going to Home Depot tomorrow to get a new mailbox. Better yet, he would give it to Trevor. The kid could probably make it like new again.

Tom sorted through the junk mail while Jip lay under the table at his feet. "Well Jip, you and I can hang out a little longer. But then I have to leave you for dinner. I'm going to meet my friend Carol for some real food. Don't worry though—I'll bring you home a treat."

Just then he heard pounding at the back door. Trevor was peeking through the glass. "Come in!" Tom shouted.

Trevor burst through the door, "Okay, Mr.T, I need a big favor."

"I've told you a million times you don't need to knock kid."

The kid was panting like he had just run a marathon, "Yeah, okay. I just need to borrow your car."

Well, this was a first. The kid always rode his bike— always. He liked to call Tom's Grand Marquis, the "Grand Polluter". He supposed Trevor was like a lot of kids of his generation—wanting to save the planet from ignorant old coots like him. He liked to remind Tom of little facts he had learned, like a cloth diaper takes five years to decompose, but today's plastic diapers take five hundred years. He had to admit, that one was pretty compelling. But Tom wasn't in the business of buying diapers—yet. And if God forbid, that day ever came, he sure as hell wasn't wearing cloth!

Tom suddenly remembered his date with Carol and frowned, "Hmm…you know anytime I would say yes kid, but wouldn't you know it, I actually need it tonight."

Trevor's face fell. "Really? No offense Mr.T but why would you need it? You never go anywhere after like four o'clock."

That was pretty much true. "I know but I actually have a date tonight with Carol."

"The noodle lady? Seriously?" Trevor looked amused. "What if I drop you off at dinner? Then I'll pick you up a couple hours later."

Wow, the kid really was desperate. Tom had a feeling this had something to do with the girl. "Well, maybe I should ask you what you need it for. That would be a start."

"Well…I have a date too, sort of." Was the kid blushing? This was a side of Trevor he had never seen before, and it was refreshing.

"Really? Let me guess, a pretty little brunette with a fancy car?"

Trevor started to ramble. He told Tom about the dinner invitation, and how she lived up in Harbor Village. Yes, she was rich, but not snobby. She was smart, nice, and hot. "Or in your language, Mr.T, she's a looker," he explained.

"Okay slow down. How about I drive you to her house and then pick you up later? Carol and I are going to dinner downtown, so it's too far to be dropping us off."

Trevor seemed to relax a bit, "Yeah, I guess that should work. But when are you going, because I told Bea I would be there soon—like around six."

"'Bea'? What's that short for? Beatrice, Betty? Or maybe beautiful? Huh?" He nudged Trevor with his elbow.

"Mr.T you can be so cheesy sometimes. Her name is Barbara but she doesn't like it."

Tom chuckled, "I see. Well no worries kid. I will get you there by six o'clock sharp. You can always count on me." And that was the God's honest truth.

***

The doorbell rang and Lorene shouted, "Bea! I think he's here!" Bea had been primping in the bathroom for over an hour. It could be another hour if Lorene didn't get the girl out of there. She tapped on the bathroom door. "Hurry it up Bea. They're here."

Lorene went to the front door and opened it. To her surprise there were three people standing there—a teenage boy and an elderly couple. "Hello! Come in, come in." She motioned them in and then focused her attention on the young one, "You must be Trevor."

He was a handsome boy with sandy brown hair and light brown eyes. He looked scared silly and just nodded.

The older gentlemen extended his hand to her. "Hello, I'm Tom Tyminski and this is my friend Carol."

"Well it's so nice to meet all of you. I've got a wonderful dinner planned. Bea will be out any minute. You know how girls can be." Carol nodded knowingly, while Tom and Trevor looked like they didn't have a clue.

"Can I get you something to drink? Soda, juice, maybe something stronger, Tom and Carol?"

Trevor finally spoke, "No, they're not staying. Well, Mr.T has other plans. But he wanted to meet Bea before he took off."

Just then Bea emerged from the bathroom. She looked especially pretty in a light blue shift dress that matched her eyes. They all made their introductions and then Tom took Bea's hand and kissed it. "You are just as lovely as Trevor told me you were." At that, the boy's face turned crimson.

"I wish we could stay, but we have reservations we don't want to miss. It was nice to meet you both." Tom said.

Lorene showed Tom and Carol to the door and then she got dinner on the table. They sat down to a feast of spinach stuffed shells, garden salad and Italian bread dipped in olive oil. Lorene even offered them each a small glass of merlot. She figured these kids could use something to help them relax. Both Trevor and Bea were quiet, and Lorene found herself initiating most of the conversation. Getting those two to say anything was like pulling teeth. She asked polite questions, and got short answers.

Thankfully, as the dinner progressed, everyone began opening up a little more. Lorene learned all about Trevor's workshop, the 'Box' as he called it. She heard about how talented he was from Bea, who was overflowing with compliments.

Lorene had to admit, she was very impressed with the boy. How could she not be? Giving away all that stuff, and visiting the children at the Haven House. Not many kids today were unselfish like that. It seemed like the youth today just wanted more, actually expected more.

She was a little concerned about his family life though. She had learned he lived with his uncle, and judging from the way the boy spoke about him, Lorene could tell Trevor didn't care for him much. But there was no mention of his parents, or any other family for that matter. The boy seemed very alone; much like Bea in a way. Maybe Tom was that one person that Trevor counted on, just as she was the one person Bea counted on.

After dinner they had ice cream sundaes with all the toppings. Trevor might've been a vegetarian, but he certainly seemed to be a good eater. He had two helpings at dinner and one of the biggest ice cream sundaes Lorene had ever seen. They all cleaned up in the kitchen together and Lorene decided it was time to say goodbye. "I hope to see you again soon Trevor." And she truly meant that.

"Yea, me too Lorene," he said smiling.

All in all, it was a very pleasant evening. Lorene could only hope the best for those two kids. She picked up her purse and her bag of leftovers, and was out the door.

CHAPTER 12

Trevor could definitely see why Bea considered Lorene her best friend. She was down-to-earth and very friendly. She really knew how to make people feel comfortable.

Finally it was just him and Bea—alone. He was feeling things he had never felt before: excitement, nervousness, and anticipation all rolled into one. The more time he spent with her, the more he thought about kissing her, holding her, touching her...

After Lorene had left, they walked out onto the back terrace. Trevor was amazed again. The stone terrace was enormous, jutting out to the edge of the lake. Wrapped around the banister were thousands of tiny twinkle lights, creating a glowing boundary between them and the endless water. To the west, the setting sun had turned the sky into wild shades of pink and orange. To the east, the

Cleveland skyline sparkled far off in the distance. Trevor could never imagine being able to come out here every night and enjoy this view. This truly was a different world.

A minute of silence passed before Trevor got the nerve to turn and face her. He had been thinking about kissing her all night. What if she freaked out again? He felt like a nervous idiot, but he didn't want to screw it up. It was now or never.

He put his arms around her waist and pulled her closer to him. "You're really pretty, you know that?" *Oh God, did he just say that?*

She obviously didn't mind, because she leaned into him, and the next thing he felt was her lips on his. Her mouth was so soft and warm… She was kissing him!

Without thinking, his body seemed to take over. He wrapped his arms around her back and kissed her more deeply. He felt a little dizzy as her body pressed against his.

He began working his way down her neck, kissing all of the soft skin he could find. It seemed to come naturally now. He found his hands sliding under her sweater and working their way up her back.

Unfamiliar sensations shot through his body and he could feel his self-control slipping away. He wanted more. He couldn't help himself.

Suddenly she pulled away from him. "Trevor, I think maybe we should take it slower, you know." Her face was flushed and her eyes were on the ground.

At that moment, a breeze of lake air hit him in the face and he seemed to snap back to reality. *Shit.* He came on too strong. "I'm sorry."

"No, it's not you. I'm sorry…God this is embarrassing." She wouldn't look at his face.

"No I'm sorry, really." This was torture. Why couldn't he be satisfied with just a kiss? He grabbed her hand, "Hey, do you want to watch a movie or something?"

She looked relieved, "Yeah, okay."

He led her back into the house. They got comfortable on the couch and starting flipping through the channels on the big screen. He felt like a jack-ass and just hoped he hadn't ruined everything.

"The Avengers" was the movie of choice. Trevor watched the super heroes fly around saving the world, but he wasn't really interested. Maybe it was the Black Widow in her tight bodysuit, but all he could think about was kissing Bea, and kissing her more…

She was curled up next to him under a big fluffy blanket. Giant pillows on both sides of the couch seemed to swallow them up. He could just lean over and…*Stop it Trevor.* He had to get it out of his head.

She put her head on his shoulder and he suddenly felt exhausted. He would just rest his eyes for a minute. Trevor wasn't sure when it happened, but they both fell asleep.

***

He had the nightmare again. Trevor was flying, and the man-in-black was chasing him. He was falling fast this time. Suddenly the man grabbed him and started shaking him. He couldn't get away. "No!" he thrashed out, trying to free himself.

"Wake up! Trevor wake up!" He was jolted awake to see Bea standing in front of him. "Trevor, you have to get up. My mom's home."

Oh no. He suddenly realized where he was. What time was it? Trevor sat up on the couch adjusting his eyes to the light.

Standing next to Bea was a woman dressed in white. As she came into focus, he realized she was wearing some kind of lab jacket. The name "Garden of Eve" was embroidered in fancy black letters on her left shoulder. She was tall and thin, maybe even taller than him, and had long, blond hair. She was the woman in the portrait, and she was very attractive.

"Hi, I'm Evelyn Stewart, Barbara's mother," she said in a cool voice. The woman oozed sophistication and confidence. Her eyes seemed to bore into him. He wasn't quite sure how to read this lady. He instantly felt uncomfortable, and a little intimidated.

His eyes quickly went to the floor. "Hi, I'm Trevor."

"Well Trevor, Barbara tells me you guys had a nice dinner. She said a friend of yours was supposed to pick you up?"

Mr. Tyminski—where the hell was he? "Yeah, my neighbor. What time is it?"

"Past midnight." Bea answered. She was chewing on her nails looking extremely uncomfortable.

"Well, I'm not sure what happened. My neighbor should've been here." Trevor said. He was a little worried now. There was no way Mr.T would've forgotten him.

Evelyn Stewart picked up her coat and turned to Bea. "All right, I'll have to take Trevor home then. Barbara, I want you to go straight to bed. You have to be up early tomorrow."

Bea walked away quickly and didn't say a word. At the top of the stairs she gave him a little wave and an apologetic look. Trevor waved back.

Then he followed Evelyn out the door.

CHAPTER 13

"He said he thought it was just heartburn at first. But then it didn't go away," Carol was babbling to one of the doctors in the emergency room.

Tom was laid out on a gurney with all kinds of monitors hooked up to him. He had made quite a first impression on their date tonight—that was for sure. After three bites of his porterhouse steak, he started feeling pain in his chest. He told Carol it was probably just indigestion, but this felt different. He didn't want to alarm her so he excused himself and went to the men's room. While splashing cold water on his face, he suddenly felt like he couldn't catch his breath. He hurried back to the table and told Carol he thought maybe they should go to the hospital, just as a precaution.

The doctors told him he had a non-segment myocardial infarction, or a mild heart attack. As if there was such a thing. They told him he would be okay; at least no surgery was necessary now. But he was going to have to take more pills and change his diet. They also said a daily walk around the block would be helpful.

Tom just nodded, but what he was thinking was that it would be a cold day in hell before he started eating healthy and exercising. At this age, what was the point? After the lecture, they told him he would have to stay in the hospital overnight for observation.

He hated being here. Just the sounds of the monitors and the smells of antiseptic brought back unpleasant memories. He had spent many days next to Maddie's bedside at this very hospital.

Carol walked over, "Hey, how you feeling?" There was obvious concern in her eyes and it was strangely comforting. "Can I get you anything?"

"Oh, I'm fine. They said it wasn't serious. I should be able to go home tomorrow." Suddenly he remembered Trevor—Tom was supposed to pick him up at that girl's house. "Oh shoot! I forgot about the kid! Could you call him and let him know what happened?"

"Of course. Oh my, he's probably worried sick by now. I'll call him right away," she jotted down the number and wandered off in search of a pay phone. Tom would make sure to let Trevor know he was *not* the only person on the planet without a cell phone.

"And make sure you say it wasn't serious! I don't want the kid to worry about me!"

"Sure thing!" Carol shouted back.

An ER nurse came over to wheel Tom to his room. As he closed his eyes, he thought about the kid. Maybe Trevor was able to get a ride from Lorene. He just hoped the poor kid wasn't walking home.

***

They drove in silence for the first few minutes. Trevor was busy examining the interior of her Mercedes. It was sweet, definitely top-of-the-line. It had all of the luxuries: heated leather seats, moon roof, navigation system, Bose stereo…all the gadgets.

And Evelyn Stewart fit right into her surroundings. This lady was high-class all the way. Everything about her was polished. Her blond hair was pulled back tightly from her well made-up face. Her bright red lipstick matched her bright red nails. The rock on her wedding ring was so big, it looked like her boney finger would snap under the weight of it.

"So how do you like Westwood Trevor?" she asked quietly.

How did she think he liked Westwood? It was a shithole compared to Harbor Village. "How do I like it? Hmm… I guess it's okay Mrs. Stewart."

She was looking him over. "Please, just call me Evelyn," she said without a hint of emotion. They drove a few more minutes in silence. He just wished she would put on the radio or something. "Can I ask you something Trevor?"

He felt a flicker of uneasiness creep up inside of him. "Sure."

"Do you think I'm attractive?" *Holy shit.* His heart started racing. He shifted in his seat turning towards the window. *What the hell should he say?*

"Yeah, I think you are attractive Mrs.—I mean Evelyn." He tried to sound as casual as possible, but he had a feeling he was failing big-time.

She spoke in almost a whisper, "You know, I work really hard to look this way. I run on the treadmill every night; I eat like a rabbit." Her voice was starting to crack. "I get facials and manicures—you name it—I do it. And, I'm a successful business woman for Christ's sake."

What the...? Trevor cautiously glanced over at her. She was about to lose it—he could feel it.

She took a tissue out of her pocket and wiped her eyes. "I don't know why I even care if that bastard is having an affair!"

Now she was swerving a little. Was she drunk? He could see her hands shaking on the steering wheel. Trevor did not like where this was going. She needed to calm down. The last thing he needed was to get in an accident with this head case.

Suddenly the car swerved sharply toward the median. "Evelyn, maybe we should pull over somewhere, like take a breather?"

She wiped her eyes with her sleeve. Black shit was streaming down her cheeks. "Okay. Yeah, I'm sorry."

She pulled into a strip mall and drove around to the back of the buildings. She parked near some trees and shut off the engine. "I am *so* sorry about that," she said sighing. "You've got to think I'm a complete nut. I just need a minute."

A wave of relief washed over Trevor. Maybe she wasn't a total psycho. He felt a sudden pang of sympathy for her. "No, no…absolutely not. You *should* be pissed. Your husband is a complete jackass if he's having an affair. Seriously."

She laughed and gave him a look that sent his blood rushing. Even with all the black shit on her face, she was still hot. And she looked so young when she let her guard down. She could pass for Bea's big sister, instead of her mom.

As Bea entered his mind, he quickly looked away. "Do you have proof? I mean do you know for sure?"

Evelyn was searching for something in her purse. "There were little signs at first. Then Lorene found this earring in the house." She held up a little gold ball. "It isn't mine or Barbara's."

Again, the mention of Bea made him squirm in his seat, "Maybe it belongs to one of Bea's friends."

Evelyn sighed, "Maybe. But you know what Trevor? A woman just knows. When you've been married to someone for twenty years, you know."

She leaned over him and reached into the glove compartment. "Excuse me. I think I have some tissues in here." She was just inches from his face and she smelled so good. His heart started racing. He closed his eyes, as if not looking at her would help anything.

And then it happened. In a matter of seconds, her lips were on his. Her very experienced mouth took complete control. He sat there motionless, eyes closed, hands at his sides. She held the sides of his face and kissed him more deeply. He didn't move.

Then she got on top of him, and her hands started pulling at his shirt. He was so turned on and so scared at the same time. He couldn't seem to move his body, but his thoughts ran wild. *Was this lady mental? What about Bea?*

"Wait…Evelyn…this is crazy…"

She started kissing his neck, her hands unbuttoning his shirt. She was whispering in his ear, "I just want to feel beautiful…I just want to feel loved and wanted. That's all I want."

The heat was building up inside of him and Trevor thought he might explode. *Get a grip!*

She ran her hands over his chest and nibbled on his ear, "Is that too much to ask? You want me, don't you Trevor?"

He grabbed Evelyn's shoulders and pushed her away. "No…this is wrong. This is really wrong." He wanted to say Bea's name but he found himself holding back. *Just say it Trevor.*

Evelyn looked him in the eyes. As if reading his mind she said softly, "Trevor, listen to me. No one will ever know. Do you hear me? Ever. But you have to decide…"

They stared at each other for seconds that seemed like minutes. And then she asked, "So Trevor, what do you want to do?"

CHAPTER 14

Trevor had tossed and turned most of the night, barely sleeping at all. No need for an alarm; he was awake well before six. The sky outside was just turning from grey to hazy white and he was ready to leave.

He wanted to get to the hospital first thing in the morning. Carol's voicemail had said Mr.T was okay, that there was nothing to worry about, but Trevor had to see for himself.

He pedaled his bike east toward the hospital trying not to think about the night before. The whole thing seemed surreal. Maybe it had all been just a dream. He arrived at the hospital and locked up his bike near the entrance doors.

At the front desk, he asked for Tom Tyminski's room and then took the elevator up to the third floor. Trevor did not like hospitals—the smell alone was as bad as Uncle Gary's laundry. He tried not to breathe through his nose.

He wandered down the hall, following the signs until he came to room 312. He peeked inside and found Mr.T in bed. Blending right into the white hospital sheet tucked under his arms, the old man looked alarmingly pale and thin. Trevor took a deep breath.

The TV was playing quietly in the background, but Mr.T appeared to be sleeping. Trevor sat in the chair next to the bed and glanced up to see the Discovery Channel on—something about black holes in the universe.

"So how was your date last night kid?"

Trevor jumped half out of his seat. "Jesus, Mr.T! I thought you were sleeping. You scared the crap out of me."

Mr.T's eyes were still closed but there was a smirk on his face. "Sorry I scared you."

An overwhelming sense of relief came over Trevor. "Well, I guess I should be asking you how your date went. Obviously not great, since you ended up in the hospital."

At this Mr.T opened his eyes and smiled. "Ha Ha. They said it was a minor heart attack. I'm just waiting for the doctor to come and give me the okay to go home."

Trevor sat up in his chair. "Heart attack? Carol told me it was an ulcer."

"I told her not to worry you kid. I'm fine really. They told me to change my diet, blah, blah."

Mr.T proceeded to tell Trevor about the dinner, having the chest pain, and thinking it was indigestion.

Trevor felt a knot forming in his stomach. He knew Mr.T was getting up there, but he couldn't imagine what life would be like without him.

Mr.T must have sensed his worry, "Really kid, it's nothing. I want to hear more about your night. Anything good happen?" He lifted his eyebrows up and down.

Trevor hesitated. He wasn't sure how to answer this. Up to this point he had been pretty honest with Mr.T. But that was probably because he never asked any tough questions. He always minded his own business and didn't get too personal.

Trevor took a deep breath. "I think I need to end things with Bea. I've only known her a few days, and things are getting way too complicated, way too fast. I just can't deal with all the drama anymore."

A frown came over Mr.T's face, "Really? What's the drama?"

Trevor closed his eyes and just decided to spill it. He couldn't keep something this big bottled up inside. "Bea's mom came onto me last night," he blurted out.

He tried to gauge Mr.T's reaction, but to his surprise, the old man showed no reaction at all. Trevor waited, "Well? Aren't you going to say something?"

Mr.T suddenly burst into laughter, "Are you pulling my leg?"

Trevor sighed, "No, I'm serious. And it's all your fault."

"Oh really! Do tell!" Mr.T's eyes sparkled. He was loving this.

"Evelyn had to give me a ride home when you didn't show."

"Ooooh, Evelyn?" Mr.T chuckled. "So I see we're on a first name basis."

Trevor fell back into his chair, "Mr.T this is serious!"

Mr.T stopped smiling, "Okay kid, no more joking—promise. So, what happened? Did you…you know?"

"No! She just came on really strong and I told her it was wrong, and she took me home. That's it."

Mr.T looked disappointed, "That's it?"

Trevor didn't want to talk about it anymore, "That's it."

CHAPTER 15

Bea had been crying. Lorene could tell as soon as she came in the door. She had just picked up the dry cleaning and was in a hurry to get dinner started. Bea was lying on the couch, staring out the window. Her eyes were red and puffy and the expression on her face said it all. This couldn't be good; Bea didn't cry very often.

Lorene walked over and sat on the couch next to her, "Bea honey, what's going on?"

"I don't want to talk about it," she said quietly.

Bea didn't need to say anymore. Lorene knew this had to be about the boy. She handed Bea a box of tissues. "Please talk to me Bea. Is it about Trevor?"

Bea reached down into her bag that was lying on the floor and pulled out her cell phone. "I got this voicemail from him today." She pushed the voicemail button and put it on speaker so Lorene could hear. It wasn't a long message; Trevor simply said he didn't think it was going to work out between them. It wasn't anything Bea did; it was all him. He thought it best if they didn't talk anymore. It was short and to the point.

Lorene wouldn't have expected something like this coming from Trevor. Based on meeting him Monday night, she thought he really liked Bea. But she guessed there was a lot about the boy she didn't know.

"Can you believe him? He just calls and leaves a voicemail—with no explanation. Can't even face me." Bea walked over to the fridge and took out a Diet Coke. "I called him yesterday because I hadn't heard from him after the dinner. Then I sent him a text just saying I wanted to talk. He didn't send anything back."

She took a sip of her soda, "I just don't get what I did. We had a good time Monday night. I thought everything was fine. I just wonder if my mom freaked him out."

"Your mom?" *When did Mrs. Stewart enter the picture?* Lorene wondered.

"Yeah, it was really bad. Trevor's friend, Mr.Tyminski, never showed. Mom had to drive Trevor home. Talk about embarrassing."

Things were starting to make a little more sense now. Lorene could definitely see Mrs. Stewart telling Trevor to keep his distance. He was from Westwood after all.

Lorene tried to offer her best advice, "Sometimes people just make rash decisions. I can tell you one thing. If it's meant to be, he'll come back to you Bea. Don't you go chasing after him."

Bea cracked a weak smile and Lorene figured that was probably the best she was going to get. She took a skillet out of the cupboard and placed it on the stove, "Now what would you like for dinner?"

***

Trevor didn't like Thursdays. On Tuesdays and Thursdays, instead of first period study hall, he had gym. He wasn't athletic in the first place and who in the hell wanted to run around at seven-thirty in the morning? He also had his sessions with Dr. Fisher on Thursdays. And this Thursday in particular really sucked because he had just broken things off with Bea.

He purposely called her mid-morning, hoping she was in class and he would get her voicemail. It worked, and he was able to leave her a really lame message without having to talk to her.

Trevor tossed his books in his locker and stuffed his sweatshirt into his backpack. He headed toward the exit when he heard Mrs. Dixon behind him, "Trevor, can I see you for a second?"

Mrs. Dixon was one of the high school guidance counselors and a major pain in his ass. Trevor turned around and waited for her to catch up. She hobbled down the hall waving a yellow paper in her hand. "Just a minute!"

This was the last thing he needed. He sighed, "I've already told you, I'm done talking to the guidance counselors."

"Oh, it's not about that." She needed to lose some weight in a bad way, and now she was almost out of breath. "The SAT scores are in and you scored the highest in the school. Let me show you." She pointed to the yellow paper, "Let's see here…" she scanned the paper with her chubby finger, "Here! Here is your score. That's good enough for most Ivy League schools Trevor. Congratulations!"

"Thanks." He thought he had done well. No real surprise there. School had always been pretty easy for him. Good skin and a high IQ—two things he guessed he had his parents to thank for. Two very important things he realized, but pretty much the only things.

He turned and headed to the door. Mrs. Dixon yelled after him, "Well Trevor, have you thought about college anymore? With your grades and these scores, you could probably get some kind of scholarship!"

He just kept walking to the door.

***

The Beaumont Mental Health Center, a.k.a. the Crazy Kids Center was recently voted the number two facility in the country for pediatric mental health. Trevor only knew this because there were billboards all over the place proudly stating the fact.

The building itself was pretty cool. It rose about ten stories high and was constructed mostly of glass. The front entrance opened into a large two-story atrium, and had a very modern feel.

An enormous fish tank stood in the middle of the atrium. It was cylindrical in shape and surrounded by high cushioned seating. Trevor loved the aquarium. It was filled with the most fantastic sea creatures: clown fish, anemones, starfish, crabs and even an octopus. He had come to his last four sessions early just so he could sit in front of it and watch. It was mesmerizing.

He took a seat on one of the benches and gazed into the glass. He was looking for the octopus. He nicknamed her Betty but he had no idea why. She hid in the rocks a lot, and today was no exception. He was concentrating his efforts on locating Betty when he heard a woman laugh. He looked up to see Dr. Fisher.

She was on the other side of the atrium, talking to another doctor. He was an older guy, looking very professional in his white coat and well-groomed silver hair. They were standing close together—a little too close in Trevor's opinion, to be just colleagues.

Dr. Fisher actually looked like she was blushing. Her body language said she was really into this guy. It was a side of her he had never seen before and Trevor found it pretty amusing.

After a little more conversation, the man put his hand on Dr. Fisher's shoulder and then turned to leave. That's when Trevor noticed the wedding ring on the guy's finger. *Oh man, was this her husband?*

But he didn't think Dr. Fisher was married—at least she didn't wear a ring. He had checked that out in their first session. And if it wasn't her husband, then she could be flirting with a married man! *Tsk, tsk, Dr. Fisher.*

Trevor watched her walk over to the elevators and go in. He looked at his watch—3:58. He would wait a couple of minutes and then head up to her office.

He was smiling to himself. He wasn't in the greatest mood today, but maybe he could have some fun with Dr. Fisher. At least he had some material to work with if things got uncomfortable. After the last session, he started doubting whether the Home Depot gift cards were really worth it.

He knocked and she immediately opened the office door. "Hello Trevor, come on in," she motioned her hand toward the chair. No blushing smiles here—all business.

He sat down and she took her position in the chair across from him, her notepad at the ready. "So how are you doing today Trevor?"

"Okay, how are you?"

"I'm fine thank you. We started talking about your mother last time—"

"Are you married Dr. Fisher?" he interrupted.

Trevor could see the surprise in her eyes. She hesitated for a second, "Why do you ask?"

"It's a pretty common question. I was just curious."

She shifted slightly in her seat, "No, I'm not married." And then she quickly asked, "So do you want to start where we left off?"

He ignored her, "I have another question. Are you a real doctor?"

Her face immediately showed a hint of annoyance, "What do you mean by *real?*"

95

"Well, I just wondered if you were an M.D., you know an actual psychiatrist, or if you were one of those psychologists with a PhD who like to call themselves doctors." Trevor already knew the answer.

She narrowed her eyes at him and he didn't look away. She pointed to the array of diplomas and awards on the wall behind her. "I have a doctorate degree in psychology and therefore I can be addressed as doctor."

Trevor liked keeping the focus on her. He sat forward in his chair so he could see her reaction better, "See, I think that's bullshit. A doctor is someone who goes to medical school, who works in a hospital, who can prescribe meds—*that's* a doctor."

She put her pad of paper on the table next to her and folded her hands in her lap. "Well, you are entitled to your opinion, but I can recommend medication to the general practitioner if I think it should be prescribed."

"So in other words, you have to get the okay from the *real* doctor first," he said smugly. He knew he was being a jack-ass, but he was having fun.

She was actually starting to look a little ticked off. "Please address me as Sarah. No need to call me Dr. Fisher if you feel that way." Then, with a tight-lipped smile on her face, she asked, "So Trevor, have you thought at all about what *you'd* like to do when you graduate?"

He leaned back in his chair, his arms crossed in front of him. "Actually I have. I think I want to be a garbage man when I grow up."

Dr. Fisher didn't show it on her face, but he knew what she was thinking. "Really, and why is that?"

"Umm…cause I like garbage? What do you mean, why? If I said I wanted to be a quote—doctor," he motioned italics in the air for emphasis, "you wouldn't ask why. You would say 'Oh that's wonderful Trevor'."

"Actually I would ask the exact same question. I don't care what you choose as an occupation. I'm more interested in why you choose it."

Trevor liked the tit-for-tat with Dr. Fisher. "That's what you say now, but you know damn well you would look down on someone wanting to be a garbage man."

"Not true," she said simply. She was a tough one to rattle.

He was still curious about the silver-haired man in the lobby. He went on, "Yeah, you would never date a garbage man. I bet you only date the rich guys. You know, *doctors*—like you. You're probably still on the hunt for Mr. Big Bucks. I bet one of your prerequisites is that he has to make six figures. Am I right?"

Trevor was on a roll and he could see he was finally getting to her. She started tapping her pen methodically on her notepad.

He wasn't sure why he felt the need to push her buttons, but he didn't want to stop. This was so much more entertaining than answering her boring questions. The more he talked about her, the less he had to talk about himself.

"Trevor, let's talk about you. Have you thought at all—?"

He wouldn't let her finish. "You know what? I bet you go for older men—I bet you like them gray! Maybe even married, like the guy in the lobby? You know, your own little sugar daddy?"

That was it. She looked pissed. "Trevor, I don't know where all of this is coming from, but I think we should just end the session here. I'm not in the mood to sit here and be insulted. Let's just say we call it a day, okay?" She got up from her chair and walked to the door.

Mission accomplished. "So we're done here?" he asked.

She sighed, "Yes, Trevor we're done." She held the door open for him.

He expected to feel relief at those words, but for some strange reason, he found himself feeling a little bit disappointed.

He shrugged his shoulders, got up, and walked out the door.

CHAPTER 16

The last three weeks had been uneventful ones for Trevor. Junior year of high school was officially finished and summer had begun. Things had pretty much gone back to normal—well maybe not normal, but uncomplicated at least.

Bea never tried to get in touch with him after he left the voicemail, which was kind of disappointing. He knew he needed to leave her alone, but he still missed her and wondered what she was up to. Did she hang out at the beach? The pool? Did she wear a bikini?

She was probably royally pissed at him. He felt bad about ending things the way he did, but he couldn't tell her face-to-face that it was over. He didn't have the guts. She would want to know why, and he didn't know what the hell to say.

Evelyn Stewart was a problem—or as he liked to call her—Evil Lyn. She had actually called Trevor a couple of times and left crazy messages about needing to talk to him. She must've gotten his number from Bea's phone.

That lady had serious issues. She always sounded half-drunk and he had no interest in hearing anything she had to say. He just wanted to forget that night ever happened.

He stayed busy working in the Box. He had picked up some valuable things at the old lady's house Frank had told him about. An old generator and a pretty decent lawnmower were two things he fixed up and gave to Uncle Gary. Hopefully, that would keep the fat-ass off his back for a while.

He had also stopped going to his appointments with Dr. Fisher at the Crazy Kids Center. He couldn't deal with that either. Down deep he felt bad about the things he had said to her. Making her sound like a gold-digger, when she had obviously worked very hard for her career, was pretty low. And he knew Mr.T wasn't happy about it. But Trevor told him he needed a break. Maybe he would go back some day, but not now.

Today was the Regional Environmental Fair for all of the Cleveland area high schools. Trevor had been working on a presentation for Westwood High on garbage recycling. Specifically he had put together a display on how many household items thrown out in the trash could actually be donated and fixed. He had photographs of many of the projects he had done in the Box.

The fair was being held at the convention center downtown. He had asked Mr.T to go with him. Trevor had a lot to carry, including one of those big tri-fold display boards. Trying to take all that stuff on the bus was going to be a pain in the ass. Mr.T was happy to help. He said he had been feeling much better since his trip to the hospital and would like to get out of the house for a change of scenery.

They walked into the main hall of the convention center and were immediately hit with the clamoring of hundreds of excited high school students. The huge room was filled with rows of long tables draped in white. Students were setting up their displays, some very elaborate, some very simple. Trevor figured his display would definitely fall on the simple side.

Some local businesses actually gave out cash prizes for things like "The Most Creative" and "The Most Feasible" exhibits. There were only two rules: the idea had to have a direct impact on the environment in a positive way. And of course, the materials used in the exhibit should be environmentally friendly. Trevor didn't really care about the prizes. He just loved to see all of the different ideas. Although, he guessed it could be pretty impressive on a college application to win something at the environmental fair.

"Wow, this is kind of crazy," Trevor said as he surveyed the room.

"Do you know where your school is?" Mr.T asked.

"Yeah, I have this map of the exhibit floor. According to this, Westwood High is towards the

Northwest corner. That way." He pointed over to the corner opposite the entrance.

They walked through the myriad of tables and projects strewn all over the floor. Finally they came to a table with a simple white curtain behind it and a small sign that read "Westwood High" in black letters. Trevor was the only person representing his school. No one else had shown any interest in attending the fair. He guessed that spending a summer afternoon raising awareness for the environmental plight of the planet, wasn't on the high list for most students at Westwood.

Trevor and Mr.T began setting up the display for his exhibit "Trash is Treasure." His tri-fold display board was like a miniature version of his photo wall in the Box. Pictures of his 'before and after's covered the board, with captions underneath showing details of when the items were restored.

Pulling open a large brown bag, Trevor began taking out small items he was able to fix up: a lamp from the seventies, an antique mirror, and an oscillating fan. He wanted to show the variety of items he found.

"When does this shindig officially start?" Mr.T asked.

"Actually I think one o'clock is when the judges come in and then it opens to the public at—." Trevor stopped in mid-sentence.

"What is it?"

She was there. One row in front of his, but at the opposite end of the convention center, stood Bea. She was standing behind a booth with a giant planet earth hanging above it.

"It's Bea," said Trevor. He couldn't stop staring at her. She hadn't seen him; he was sure of it.

Just then, a tall blond guy dressed in khakis and a navy jacket walked over to Bea and stood next to her. *Didn't Bea go to an all-girl's school?*

As soon as Trevor finished the thought, Blondie was putting his arm around her and whispering something in her ear. She was laughing. A strange feeling was creeping over Trevor and he didn't like it. "What the…?"

Mr.T chimed in, "Oh yes, I see her now…"

"You know what? I'm gonna go say 'hi'…yeah, I'll be back in a minute." Without thinking, Trevor quickly walked over to Bea's table, never taking his eyes off her. He didn't want to lose his nerve.

He was only a couple of steps away when she looked up and saw him. Her eyes got wide and she immediately stopped smiling.

"Hi Bea."

Crossing her arms in front of her, she met his eyes with an intense stare. No response.

Shit, what was he thinking? Too late now…

He stumbled on his words, "I, uh…I didn't know you would be at the fair." *Real smooth.*

She waved her hand toward Blondie. "This is Kevin, my boyfriend. Kevin, this is an old friend of mine, Trevor." She made the introduction with a phony smile.

Her words stung and Trevor felt his face getting hot. His eyelid started twitching. He couldn't believe it—was this guy really her boyfriend? And why did that bother him so much? He looked at Bea, trying to figure out what to say next.

"I'm sorry, did you say Ken? Like Ken and Barbie?" He couldn't hide his anger. "That's cute. How long has Ken here been your boyfriend?"

Blondie spoke up with a hint of fear in his voice, "It's Kevin, and we just met two weeks ago. Honest."

Bea leaned over the table and said, "You know what Trevor? It's none of your business. We're not friends anymore. You blew me off, remember?" She turned to Kevin, "I'll be back later."

As Bea walked away from the booth, Trevor frantically tried to think of something to say, but she was gone before he could.

Trevor and Kevin were left standing there staring at each other. Kevin just shrugged his shoulders, "Sorry, man."

"Yea whatever." Trevor walked back to his booth feeling frustrated and defeated.

CHAPTER 17

Trevor was definitely upset; the kid was quiet for the rest of the fair. His enthusiasm seemed to disappear and it wasn't hard to figure out why. Tom caught him looking over at the girl's booth several times, but she didn't seem fazed by their earlier meeting. She was laughing and carrying on with another boy. Tom was sure it was eating Trevor up inside. Ah, young love…

During the drive home Tom tried to cheer the kid up. He told Trevor an embarrassing story about a recent visit to his cardiologist. At his last check-up Tom asked the doctor if it would be safe for him to take Viagra. After all, he and Carol had been spending a lot of time together and who knows what could happen. And he wasn't a spring chicken anymore, that was for sure. He might need some help in that department.

"And guess what he said?" Tom looked over at Trevor who simply stared straight ahead. "He said it was too risky now. I was so ticked off."

Tom was determined to get a reaction out of the kid, "Well, the doctor could see my disappointment, so he told me a good joke to cheer me up. You want to hear it?"

Trevor sighed, "Sure."

"Okay see, an old man is putting on his coat and his wife asks where he is going. He tells her he's going to the doctor to get some Viagra. So the wife gets up and puts on her coat and the husband asks where she is going."

Tom chuckled to himself, but the kid's expression hadn't changed. "And the wife says she is going to the doctor too. And the husband is confused and he says 'Why?' and she says 'Because if you're going to start using that rusty old thing again, I'm going to get a tetanus shot.'"

The kid finally smiled—barely, but it was still a smile. "Good one, huh?"

After a few more minutes of silence Tom prodded, "So, you really like that girl, Bea?"

Trevor's eyes were still on the road, "Yeah, I guess I like her more than I thought I did. Seeing her with that Kevin dork really pissed me off."

"You know it's never too late to say you're sorry. I'm sure she would go out with you again if you asked. I think she was just putting on a show with that other guy."

Trevor laughed, "Mr.T. I think you're forgetting something. Her mom...all the drama. It's just messy."

The kid had a point, but Tom could also see he had it bad for this girl. "Well you'll figure it out kid."

Trevor shrugged his shoulders. "And, what's the point, you know? I mean we only have one more year of high school and then who knows what we'll be doing. She just gets under my skin. I mean you can't really be serious about someone at my age."

Trevor got off the highway and they started driving toward Westwood. "God, I'm hungry, I think there's a Subway up here."

"You're wrong Trevor," Tom said.

"What? No Subway?"

"No. You're wrong about being serious with someone at your age. I met my wife when I was seventeen. You can definitely be serious with someone. You can even find the love of your life. I'm not trying to give you false hope, but it does happen."

"Mr.T...Can I ask how long you were married?"

Tom had a hard time saying it, "Thirty-two years."

"Wow, that's a long time."

It should've been much longer, thought Tom. "Yeah, they were thirty-two great years."

"And you have two daughters that live in California, right?"

Both of Tom's daughters, now in their forties, lived in San Diego. Both were happily married and had successful careers. They had moved there shortly after graduating from college. They bothered Tom continuously about moving out there—especially after Maddie died.

Even though the weather was a perfect sunny seventy-two degrees every day, Tom couldn't find it in his heart to leave Cleveland. He would visit the girls often, and loved it for a week or two, but no more than that. As crazy as it may sound, the palm trees and fancy cars just weren't for him.

"Yep, two wonderful daughters, and three wonderful grandchildren." Tom nudged Trevor with his elbow, "And you would've met them by now if you ever took me up on my offer."

Every summer the girls came out to visit Tom. They rented a large vacation home on Kelley's Island in Lake Erie. Tom really didn't have enough room at his house, and the islands were only an hour away from Westwood.

The whole family came, and they made it a real vacation. They cruised the lake, fished for bass, and made s'mores on the campfire. Tom looked forward to it every year, and he asked Trevor to tag along every year. And every year, the kid politely declined.

Now Tom was starting to get hungry. They were only a few minutes from home and had passed the Subway long ago. As if reading his mind, Trevor asked, "Hey, you want to go to Sorak's for some dinner?"

Tom's mouth started watering at the thought. "Now that's an idea." He was starving for some home-cooked food and he would love to see Carol. It was strange how at his age, he could still get butterflies when he saw a special lady.

Sure, Carol might be a little rough around the edges, but she had a lot of great qualities. She was a hard worker, honest, and kind. She had been widowed for the last ten years, and now that her husband was gone, she said the diner was like her family. The friends she made there kept her from ever feeling lonely. Yeah, he and Carol were good companions for each other, without a doubt.

Trevor parked in front of the diner and Tom turned to him. "Listen kid, maybe you should try one more time with the girl. Forget about all the other nonsense. It seems like you really like her. What the hay?"

"What the hay? Really Mr.T?" Trevor shook his head at Tom. "I don't know, maybe I will."

With that, they got out of the Grand Polluter and went inside to get some noodles.

CHAPTER 18

One of the most disturbing cases in recent Cleveland history, the Paula McNulty case stirred anger in even the most seasoned law enforcement officials. On that fateful day in September of 2010, police received the 911 call...

Even when Lorene saw it in print, she almost didn't believe it. Her curiosity about Trevor had finally gotten to her. A couple of days after he broke up with Bea, Lorene and Reggie looked him up on the computer. She wanted to find out something about his parents—his past—anything.

And what she found out was shocking. She had heard about the tragic story when it happened; everyone heard about it. Lorene had forgotten the name of the family involved, but she never forgot the case. She could only say a prayer for him now, and hope the best for him. *My God, that poor kid.*

The last three weeks had been quiet ones at the Stewart house, but not necessarily quiet in a good way. Bea was depressed, there was no doubt about that. Lorene hadn't seen the girl smile even once. This was Bea's first real crush and she was already emotionally fragile, so this reaction didn't surprise Lorene.

What did surprise Lorene, was how she found herself feeling lately. She couldn't get Trevor McNulty out of her head. Here was this boy, who came from a horrible upbringing and experienced things that should never be inflicted on a child. Then he had to live with the only family he had—an uncle who seemed to be a real piece of work.

And what did Trevor do? Did he turn to drugs, or a life of crime? No, he did the exact opposite. He did something more generous than most of the privileged kids in Bea's high school would ever do—he gave to others.

Lorene walked over to shut the kitchen window. The weather was beautiful earlier, but a wicked summer storm had rolled in off the lake in a hurry. The thunder was loud and the rain was heavy.

Bea would be home soon and Lorene was curious to see how today's environmental fair went. For the past couple of weeks the fair was the only thing she seemed to care about. Bea's school always did a joint project with the Andrews Academy for Boys.

Her partner was a nice enough kid named Kevin, and they had spent a lot of time together recently. Bea said that she really liked Kevin but Lorene knew better. On a scale from one to ten, Bea's excitement level when she mentioned Kevin was about a two. When she used to talk about Trevor, it was off the charts.

As Lorene started preparing dinner, the doorbell rang. She wasn't expecting company, only Bea. She opened up the door to find a giant bouquet of orange Gerber daisies in front of her. They were wrapped in pink cellophane and battered from the heavy rain. Behind the drooping, half-ruined flowers was a very wet Trevor. He was clad in a soaked sweatshirt and ripped jeans.

She looked over his shoulder toward the driveway, and saw his bike lying in the grass. The boy rode his bike, a twenty minute car-ride from Westwood, with those flowers in tow! He looked downright pitiful.

"Come in, come in," Lorene motioned him in the door.

Trevor walked into the foyer but said nothing.

"Well Lord, you are just drenched! Here, let me take those." Lorene grabbed the bouquet out of his hands, "Hold on there, I'll be right back. Don't move." She went to the bathroom and came back with two large bath towels, and one of Bill Stewart's robes. As soon as Trevor saw the robe, his eyes got wide.

"Uh, you don't want me to wear that, do you?" He asked with slight panic in his voice.

"Look Trevor, Bea won't be home for at least an hour. You can't keep those clothes on—you'll be sick. If you didn't notice, the Stewarts like to keep the house nice and cool. In spite of the storm, the central air is still on high."

The boy took the robe but didn't move.

"I'll put your clothes in the dryer and they'll be ready in twenty minutes, okay? There's a bathroom right in that hallway, first door on your left."

He looked down the hall as if contemplating what to do. He finally reached for one of the towels and hurried to the bathroom.

Lorene put the teapot on to boil; maybe some hot chocolate might warm him up and ease his nerves.

Trevor came out of the bathroom in the plush, full-length navy robe, looking highly embarrassed. "I feel like an idiot."

Lorene tried to suppress a laugh, "Oh it's not so bad. You look very…grown-up in that." Just then the teapot started whistling. "I was just thinking about you. Would you like some hot chocolate?"

"Yeah, thanks." The boy sat down on a stool at the kitchen counter. "Will Bea's parents be coming home soon?"

"Oh no. They don't get home until much later. Marshmallows or no marshmallows?"

He looked at her with a puzzled expression, "In the hot chocolate you mean?"

"Sure, didn't your mom ever make you—?" Lorene stopped herself in mid-sentence. As soon as the words came out, she regretted it. *Damn.*

He put his head down, "No, she didn't," he said quietly.

Lorene felt her heart sink. *How could she make a mistake like that!* She tried to change the subject, "Bea had a school science fair today."

Trevor seemed to ignore her attempt at small talk, "You're probably wondering about my parents. I mean, why would I live with an uncle that I obviously can't stand?"

Lorene was unsure of what to say, "Only if you want to tell me."

He kept his eyes on his hot chocolate, "Well, my dad left a long time ago and my mom is dead. She never made me hot chocolate with marshmallows—she never did a lot of things." Lorene could hear a hint of anger in his voice.

"Trevor, I am so sorry. I didn't mean to upset you."

But it was too late. He got up and walked to the bathroom. He stopped at the door, and without turning around said, "Can I have just have my clothes please?"

"Of course." Lorene hurried to the laundry room and grabbed the damp clothes from the dryer. She wanted to kick herself for being so stupid.

After she handed the clothes to Trevor he disappeared into the bathroom. When he came out a few minutes later, his eyes were wet and his face was flushed. Oh Lord, had he been crying?

Lorene couldn't let the boy leave like that. She walked over to him, putting her hands on his shoulders as a mother would to a child. He remained rigid, standing like a statue with his eyes fixed on the ground.

"Trevor, I know about your past, okay? I know about what happened—I know about your mom. You don't ever have to talk about it, but I just want you to know, I'm your friend and I'm always here."

Lorene could see the surprise in his face, "You know everything?" he asked.

"Yes, and I'm so sorry Trevor. The truth is I admire you. I really do. You have such a beautiful spirit. Don't ever lose that spirit, you hear me?"

He nodded his head. "Are you going to tell Bea? About my mom, I mean?"

"It's not really my place. You have to do that on your own." Lorene's heart truly ached for the boy. "Now, I don't want you to run out, okay? Will you please have a seat? Bea should be here any minute. I really think you should stay."

Trevor looked at Lorene with pained eyes, "Okay. I guess I'll stay."

***

Trevor sat at the counter sipping his hot chocolate. His damp clothes were still warm from the dryer. Lorene was making some kind of sauce for the dinner she was preparing. It smelled really good, but too bad for him, it wasn't vegetarian.

He was embarrassed about what had just happened between him and Lorene. He wasn't sure why he had gotten so upset when she mentioned his mom. But at the same time he felt relieved. Lorene was the person closest to Bea and she seemed like a pretty decent lady. If she was okay with his past and didn't judge him by it, then that was something to be optimistic about.

Lorene put the dinner in the oven and turned to Trevor, "Do you want me to put those in a vase for her, or...?" She was pointing at the flowers he bought.

Mr.T told him girls always liked getting flowers. Trevor picked these orange ones because they stood out against all the rest, kind of like Bea. But now they looked pathetic.

Trevor smiled, "I know. They look pretty bad, huh?"

"No, they're beautiful, really. It's just if I put them in a vase I can rearrange them a little better, clip off some of the broken stems. It really doesn't matter, because Bea is just going to be thrilled to see you."

He felt a flutter in his chest. "You think so? You don't think she's going to be pissed I'm here?"

Lorene walked over and leaned on the counter, looking him straight in the eye. "Trevor, she likes you a lot. She would kill me for telling you this, but she's been moping around here nonstop for the last couple of weeks. I know Bea. She may not show it at first, but she will be very happy to see you."

Nice! He tried to appear nonchalant and took a sip of his hot chocolate. "Really?"

Just then the front door opened and Bea walked into the kitchen. "Hey Lorene! You'll never guess who—." She stopped in mid-sentence when she saw him sitting at the counter.

He sat up straighter in his seat and tried to look casual, "Hey Bea," he said.

God, she looked good. She had on a bright orange rain jacket with the hood pulled tight. Little wisps of her short black hair were plastered to the sides of her face.

She immediately ripped off her hood and started pushing her hair away from her face. "Hey," she said with a cool tone.

Lorene walked over to the oven and stirred the sauce. "You know what? I'm going to go check on that laundry." She hurried out of the room without turning around.

Bea stayed in the entrance, her eyes avoiding his. Trevor quickly picked up the vase and walked over to her. He tried to remember what Lorene had told him, *she doesn't hate you Trevor.*

"These are for you." He handed her the orange daisies. "They match your jacket." *Apologize idiot!*

"So what are you doing here?"

His heart pounded as he contemplated what to say. He needed to get it right. "Bea, I'm really sorry...I'm sorry I just left you a voicemail like that. I know that was really lame."

At this, she finally looked at him, "Trevor I just don't understand what happened. I know we weren't hanging out that long, but I thought we were at least friends. I thought at least we could talk about it, but you just avoided me completely."

He took the vase out of her hands and set it on the counter. Something was stirring in the pit of his stomach. "I know I was a jerk, and I'm sorry. Bea, you are my friend. And I hope we can be more."

This was all so new to him and he felt his face getting hot once again. "And you didn't do anything wrong, believe me, it was not you. I was just going through some stuff. I know that sounds cliché, but it's true."

He took a step closer and put his arms on her shoulders. "When I saw you at the fair, I realized...I guess I realized that I like you, a lot."

She smiled, "I like you too Trevor."

He didn't hesitate another second. He leaned down and kissed her, wrapping his arms around her back and holding her tight. The kiss grew more intense and he could feel everything heating up. His hands moved instinctively, down her back and under her shirt, feeling the warmth of her bare skin.

Suddenly a loud "Uh-hum" came from the hallway. They quickly pulled away from each other, both of them looking down at the floor. *Awkward.*

Lorene walked over to the stove. "Maybe Trevor would like to stay for dinner? I can make you up a vegetarian plate if you'd like," she offered.

Bea replied for him, "Actually, he wanted to know if I could give him a ride home now. It's still raining pretty hard."

He was hoping she would say that.

Lorene smiled, "Okay. Be careful you two."

He grabbed Bea's hand and they walked to the front door together. On their way out he turned around, "Hey Lorene, thanks a lot—for everything."

"Don't mention it." As Bea made her exit, Lorene gave Trevor a big thumbs-up.

CHAPTER 19

Trevor got into the passenger side of Bea's SUV. He was thinking about his earlier talk with Lorene. She told him she knew everything. *Everything?*

He really wanted to tell Bea about his past too, but he just got her back. What if she didn't understand?

"Hey, how did you guys do at the environmental fair?" Bea asked.

He laughed, "You mean Mr. Tyminski and I? I was the only one from my school that wanted to do it. We didn't win anything big. What about you guys?" Trevor didn't want to say Kevin's name.

"We did okay. We got second place in 'Best Visual Aid'."

"Cool." Silence settled in and Trevor's mind started racing. He really wanted to be alone with Bea—just go park somewhere and see what happened. But he also wanted to get some things off his chest; he wanted to be honest with her.

As if reading his mind, Bea asked, "Trevor, can I ask you a question...about your parents?"

He felt a little relieved that she had brought it up, but he didn't know exactly how to start.

She must have sensed his uneasiness, "I'm sorry, I don't know why I just asked that."

"No, it's okay, really." He had to tell her. "Umm, I think Edgecliff Park is up here. Why don't we go there and talk?"

She turned right toward the park, "You sure?"

"Yeah," The radio was playing an Imagine Dragons song. "Do you like them, Imagine Dragons?" he asked.

"I guess. Probably not my first choice, but their songs are pretty good. Do you like them?"

Trevor took his cell phone out of his sweatshirt pocket, "I know this is a ridiculously popular song, but there's something about it." He played the 'Radioactive' ringtone.

While sticking the phone back in his pocket, he noticed a new text message waiting. He didn't recognize the number and opened it up.

It's Evelyn. Will you please call this number? I really need to talk to you. Please.

Trevor flipped the phone shut. What was that lady thinking? He couldn't deal with Evelyn now. He had to concentrate on telling Bea the truth.

Looking out his window, he admired the huge oak trees that lined the drive. This park was beautiful—plenty of green space and lots of winding paths. When the weather was nice, people walked their dogs, biked, and pushed their kids in strollers. Benches were lined up along the paths and old people fed the birds.

But today the park was pretty empty. The rain had subsided, but the sky was still grey. There was a small parking lot at the end of the drive. It was edged with weeping willows on one side and a large pond on the other. Bea parked facing the pond.

"Trevor I'm sorry. You really don't have to talk about it, if you don't want to."

"No, it's okay, really. I mean I'm sure you're wondering why I live with my white trash uncle."

Trevor took a deep breath and went on, "I was seven when my dad left. I guess he had a girlfriend or something. We never heard from him—he just kind of disappeared."

He looked out across the pond. There was an elderly couple sitting on a bench together. He wondered how long they had been together.

"I don't know much about him. He was an auto worker and I guess I looked like him, because my mom always used to say 'You look just like your father'. Not in a good way though—like she was disgusted or something."

Bea reached over and grabbed his hand. It was a nice gesture, but it made him feel even more uncomfortable and he slowly pulled it away.

"My mom changed our names back to McNulty— her maiden name. I used to be Trevor Anuskiewicz.

After writing that one a few times in kindergarten, McNulty didn't seem so bad. Anyway, mom said she was better off without my dad, but she wasn't. At first, she just went out all the time—she was never home. Then, after a while, she did the exact opposite and started hiding out in her bedroom. She basically lived in there."

Trevor glanced over at Bea, unsure what to expect. She looked sad, but not surprised or appalled.

He didn't know if he could tell her anymore, "You know what? Maybe I should just stop telling you all this crap. It's in the past."

"But... what happened to your mom?"

Of course that was what she had been wondering the whole time. His eyelid twitched and he suddenly didn't feel so hot. "Can we go get some air? Maybe walk around or something?"

"Sure," she said.

With their hoods up, and hands in their pockets, they walked down the embankment to the edge of the pond. Sitting down on the grass, Trevor could feel the wetness through his jeans, but he didn't care.

"Then when I was thirteen..." his voice trailed off. The old couple across the pond got up from the bench. They walked up the path holding hands and smiling at each other like they were on a first date. He thought about Mr.T and Carol.

"Trevor?"

He couldn't tell her everything—not now. "My mom...died."

He knew he probably sounded cold-hearted, but he was trying to keep his emotions in check. He didn't want to lose it.

"God, I'm sorry Trevor."

"I didn't have anywhere to go so I lived in a children's home for a few months. Then Uncle Gary figured out he could get some money from the state, if he took me in. That idiot is my only living relative. All of the other McNulty's reside at Westwood Cemetery." He threw another stone, feeling the anger stirring inside him. "Good old Uncle Gary—he's the only one left."

Bea turned to face him. "And you." She put her arms around him and pulled him close. "I'm so sorry Trevor." The words were muffled against his shoulder.

He looked out over the green water, "Yeah, me too."

"Hey! I just thought about something!" Her voice was suddenly cheerful, "I've got this family thing tomorrow night. Would you maybe want to come? I mean, it will probably be lame, but…"

Trevor immediately thought of Evelyn. Mrs. Stewart may be more of a problem than he initially thought. "Would you be really mad if I took a rain check? I've got a ton of work to do in the Box tomorrow. My uncle's been riding me pretty hard lately."

"Sure, it's okay. No biggie, really." He could hear the disappointment in Bea's voice, but she wasn't going to push it. She must've known how hard it was for him to open up about his mom.

And, he was relieved that she seemed okay with his past. Of course, he had only told her the main points: his dad left and his mom died. And that was only a small part of a much bigger picture—a picture that was so horrible, it haunted him every day, and every night.

CHAPTER 20

The antique light fixture was probably valuable, and definitely fixable. That's what Mr.T said anyway. Trevor examined the tarnished brass base under the lights of his workstation. Electrical wiring was not his specialty, and definitely not old electrical wiring. He started searching through his screwdriver drawer for a large Philips head. If he could get it fixed, maybe Uncle Gary could sell it off to someone, and get off his case for a while.

Other than that pain in the ass, things were definitely looking up. Trevor really thought him and Bea might have a chance. After their talk in the park yesterday, she took him home and they kissed each other goodbye. Trevor invited her into the Box, but she said she had to get up really early. He didn't know if she was blowing him off or not, but he was okay with taking things slow. The last thing he wanted to do was screw things up with Bea again.

It was Saturday night and she was busy with the family thing, so he decided to hang out in the Box. Mr.T had taken Carol out to dinner. Those two were quite the item; Trevor was happy for him.

He carefully unscrewed the bottom of the light fixture and looked at the web of old wires. Maybe he would just work on this tomorrow when Mr.T could help.

Just then Jip started barking. He heard a car pulling into the gravel driveway. Maybe Uncle Gary decided he'd had enough of the Barley Tavern scene. That was doubtful though. It was only around eight, and he never came home before midnight on a Saturday.

Trevor opened the door to the Box and peeked out. It was dark and he had to look twice—but there was no mistaking it. Parked in his driveway was a silver Mercedes. *Shit.*

He closed the door quickly and stood with his back to the wall. He turned the dead bolt and tried to stay as quiet as possible. But when the car door slammed shut, Jip started barking again.

"Quiet Jip!" He whispered in his harshest tone, but it was no use. With Jip's barking and the lights shining inside the Box, she had to know he was in there.

Trevor crouched down and almost crawled over to the tiny window. Very slowly he lifted his head and peeked out into the backyard.

Like a ghost in the night, Evelyn Stewart, draped in white from head to toe, was coming toward the Box. As she got closer, Trevor's mind started racing. He put his head in his hands. *What was this lady's problem?*

He stayed down on the floor and tried not to make a sound. Maybe she would just look around and leave...

But as soon as the hopeful thought entered his mind, Evelyn started banging on the door. "Trevor! Are you in there?" *Bang, bang, bang.*

She slurred her words, "Trevor, it's me, Evelyn, will you please talk to me?" She sounded wasted.

Trevor debated about what to do next. The sad thing was, she probably wasn't going to leave unless he talked to her. *Bang, bang, bang.*

"Alright!" He slowly opened the door.

Evil Lyn stood there, wide-eyed, with a crazed smile on her face. Her hair was all messed up and she had black shit streaming down her cheeks once again. She could barely hold herself up, swaying from side to side. And she didn't smell like roses. She smelled more like Uncle Gary after a hard night at the tavern. "Hello Trevor." She fell forward into his arms.

"Whoa!" He caught her just before she landed on her face. He grabbed under her arms and pulled her into the Box. "Evelyn, what are you doing here?" He sat her down on an old garden bench he had been working on.

She could barely keep her head up, "I think I have a drinking problem Trevor. What do you think?" She began laughing hysterically.

Jesus. Trevor looked down at Jip as if he might be able to help. "You know what Jip? In my next life, I want to come back as a dog. Not have to deal with all this bullshit."

Evelyn's laughter immediately turned to tears, "I'm sorry... I came here. I'm sorry...," she wailed between muffled sobs.

He was at a loss and didn't know what the hell to say. She was so drunk, she probably wouldn't remember anything he said anyway. "Mrs. Stewart—I mean Evelyn," he kneeled down to her level and tried to look her in the face, "You have to leave me alone, okay?"

She lifted her head up slowly, looking at Trevor with glossy bloodshot eyes, "I just didn't know where else to go. I can't face anyone. You like me don't you Trevor?"

He reached over, took hold of her arm, and lifted her up by the elbow, "Nope, we're not going through this again. I'm taking you home. You need to go lie down and sober up. I'll take you. There's no way I'm letting you drive." Then he suddenly thought of Bea, "Is your family at home?"

Evelyn held on to the wall, "No. Bill took Bea out to dinner for some father-daughter time. Hah, what a joke that is. She'll be at home one more year and he decides he wants to be a father now. Typical."

"Okay, let's go then," He did his best to lead her to the car and put her into the passenger side. He threw his bike in the trunk.

He was not looking forward to riding back to Westwood this late, but he didn't have a choice. He had to get her out of there. If Uncle Gary did decide to come home early, Trevor would have a hard time explaining this one.

***

The drive to the Stewart's seemed much longer than twenty minutes. Evelyn passed out almost immediately, and in the silence Trevor had nothing to do but think. What was he going to do with this lady? He had just gotten things back on track with Bea, and now Evil Lyn was threatening it all. He had to think of some way to fix this, and soon.

As they approached the house, Trevor slowed down and shut off the headlights. They came to a stop at the end of the driveway—exactly where he and Bea first met. God, it seemed like years ago, not weeks.

Everything seemed quiet; no lights on and no cars in the driveway. He pulled up and killed the engine.

"Okay Evelyn. We're here." No response. "Wake up." He repeated it a little louder and shook her shoulder.

She finally opened her eyes and sat up, "Where am I?" She looked at Trevor with alarm on her face, obviously not having a clue where she was.

The last thing Trevor needed was Evelyn causing a scene. He said in his calmest voice possible, "You're at home. I drove you here. Do you need help getting into the house?"

She looked over at the house and realization seemed to set in. "Oh." She started pulling at the car door handle and couldn't get it open.

"Do you need some help?" he asked.

"No, no…I'm fine." Suddenly the door swung open, and she fell out, right onto the pavement. If the whole situation wasn't so serious, he would be laughing his ass off. *Mr.T, if you could only see me now.*

Trevor ran around to the other side of the car and helped her off the ground as quietly as possible. Both of her arms were wrapped around his neck, the smell of her booze breath all over him.

"All right Evelyn, let's go." He slowly began leading her up the driveway. She probably only weighed ninety pounds but it felt like much more. The entire way, she pulled down on his sweatshirt and dragged her feet while rambling off garbled apologies.

They finally made it to the front door and he pulled out her keys. The second key he tried worked and the lock clicked.

He just had to get her in the house and this nightmare would be over. But what Trevor didn't realize, as he pushed open the heavy front door, was that the biggest nightmare awaited him on the other side.

CHAPTER 21

Lorene wished that man would just shut up and have a drink already. Bill Stewart had been pacing like a caged animal, mumbling under his breath for the last twenty minutes. Lorene wasn't sure where Mrs. Stewart was, but she hoped for the sake of everyone there that she showed up soon.

Lorene had called the salon and they told her that Mrs. Stewart had left at five-thirty, over three hours ago. She should've been home by now.

Bea had purposely told her mom that she and dear old dad were going out to dinner. That way, Mrs. Stewart would think she had the house to herself. That woman loved her evenings home alone and it wasn't a secret. Lorene and Bea figured she would probably be home by seven at the latest. They were wrong.

They had been planning the surprise 40th birthday party for the last couple of weeks. Lorene thought maybe working on a party would be a good distraction for Bea. The girl had been so down-in-the-dumps lately. And because it was a full month before Mrs. Stewart's real birthday, they knew she wouldn't suspect anything.

It was a little last minute, but it was amazing what money could do. Bill Stewart's involvement was purely financial. To no one's surprise, he simply wrote a blank check and said "Tell me when and where." That was fine by Lorene and she took full advantage.

Bea made sure all of her mom's favorite things were incorporated into the party. Fresh Cymbidium orchids, Mrs. Stewart's favorite, adorned the tabletops. Overhead, thousands of white twinkle lights wrapped in tulle draping illuminated the room. An enormous swan ice sculpture sat in the middle of the buffet table. Mrs. Stewart loved swans.

With over one hundred guests, there was enough gourmet food to feed a small country and a full staff to wait on them. They had hired a harpist to play during dinner—Mrs. Stewart's favorite instrument.

No expense was spared for this party, much to Bill Stewart's dismay. Lorene had even rented a shuttle bus to transport guests from a nearby parking lot. That way, there wouldn't be any cars parked out front to tip off the party. They had gone to great lengths to make sure Mrs. Stewart was completely shocked.

Just then Bea came running from the front foyer, "Kill the lights! She just pulled in! Quick, everyone hide! Hide! Shhh!"

Lorene fumbled in the dark, holding Reggie's hand and pulling him down beside her. They were crouched behind a giant potted fern in the corner of the great room.

Only the front entryway was dimly lit and Lorene had a perfect view of it. She wasn't sure what Mrs. Stewart's reaction would be, but she hoped it would be a happy one.

CLICK

The door lock echoed through the silent room. The massive front door pushed open into the darkness. Lorene could only see a shadow. She shifted her footing, trying to get a better view of Mrs. Stewart. There was a scuffling sound and then the flick of the light switch.

All of the guests jumped to their feet and yelled "Surprise!" in a deafening roar.

Silence settled in immediately and a collective hush fell over the vast room. Lorene stared in astonishment at the scene before her. And then, in a matter of seconds, all hell broke loose.

***

Scared shitless—that was the term that came to mind as Trevor faced the crowd in front of him. A sea of wide eyes and gaping mouths stared back in horror. Hot, nauseating waves of panic surged through him and his grip on Evelyn's arm suddenly gave way. She fell to the floor in a drunken heap. *This can't be happening.*

In seconds, Bill Stewart was at her side, lifting her up and carrying her like a baby over to the couch. He laid her down and covered her with a blanket. The partygoers all looked at each other with bewilderment and confusion.

Trevor was frozen. His feet seemed to be cemented to the ground. *Oh God...* He would give anything for a giant black hole to open beneath him and swallow him—right then, right there.

Bill Stewart slowly turned to Trevor. His eyes were filled with rage, his fists clenched at his side. The man looked like he was about to go postal. Another term quickly came to mind—dead meat.

"Who in the hell are you and what have you done to my wife?!" he shouted at Trevor, his spit spraying in the air.

As Trevor's mind raced, his eyes darted across the room and that's when he saw Bea. She was standing in the middle of the room, staring at him like everyone else.

But unlike everyone else, she looked like she was about to cry. He wanted to reach out to her and start explaining. He wanted to plead with her and tell her it wasn't his fault. But his lips wouldn't move—nothing would move.

"Well!?" Bill Stewart was in front of him now, his face just inches from Trevor's, "I asked you a question!"

"I...I just..." the words wouldn't come.

"Mr. Stewart! Hold on Mr. Stewart!" A familiar voice rose up from the back of the room. All heads turned in that direction. Lorene was working her way through the crowd, "Hold on, I can explain this. Let me explain!"

Trevor had no clue where she was going with this, but he didn't care. Thank God for Lorene.

"This is my friend, Trevor." Lorene stood at his side and put her hand on his shoulder. "He rides the bus into town with me sometimes. He works at one of the restaurants here."

Trevor couldn't believe his ears. "See when Mrs. Stewart was running late, I called Trevor here and asked him if he would do a big favor for me. I asked him to go around town to some of the local establishments and see if he might be able to find her." Lorene was putting on a great performance, "Unfortunately, I failed to mention the party to him. It's my fault, not his."

Mr. Stewart actually seemed to be buying it, his red face slowly fading to pink. He glared at Trevor for only a few seconds more and then turned to the stunned spectators, "Well everyone, I don't think my wife is in the mood for a party and I don't think I am either. I sincerely apologize, and I thank you all for coming."

The guests slowly began filing out the front door. Trevor could hear their rumblings of disapproval as they gawked at him on their way out.

When the house finally emptied, only a handful of people remained: Lorene and her husband Reggie, Evelyn and Bill Stewart, and Bea, sitting in a chair on the other side of the room.

The look of hurt on her face felt like a punch in Trevor's gut. He had never seen her like that before. He wanted to run to her and tell her it was all a big mistake. But he was frozen, just like in a dream. He kept his eyes on the floor and just prayed the nightmare would be over soon. He just wanted to get the hell out of there.

Suddenly Evelyn sat up on the couch, her head swaying from side to side. She tried to stand up, but Mr. Stewart promptly sat her back down, "Evelyn, I demand to know what's going on! This behavior is ridiculous! For God's sakes, what has gotten into you?"

She fell over onto her side and buried her head in a pillow, "You! You bastard! You are what's gotten into me! I hate you!"

Mr. Stewart looked dumbfounded, but Evelyn wasn't finished. She looked up at him with her crazy eyes, "Do you hear me? I hate you!"

Trevor began back-stepping. He needed to get out of there—now.

"Only Trevor understands me!" she screamed.

Oh no. He stopped dead in his tracks. All eyes were on him in an instant.

Evelyn stood up and pointed her finger directly at Trevor. She smiled, "He's sweet and kind...and he definitely knows how to please a woman."

Shit. Trevor immediately looked over at Bea but she was already running from the room.

Bill Stewart's face turned purple, "What!? What in the hell are you talking about?" He looked at Trevor, his face full of fury. "What is she talking about?"

Evelyn broke out into hysterical laughter and shrieked, "Tell them Trevor! Tell them about our night in the Mercedes!"

His heart was beating out of his chest. He held his hands up in front of him, "Look, I don't know what she's talking about. This lady's crazy. I never—."

"You son-of-a-bitch!" Bill Stewart screamed and lunged toward him at full force.

In a flash, Trevor turned on his heel and bolted to the front door. As he tried to get it open, Bill Stewart grabbed him from behind. Trevor pulled away with every ounce of strength that he had, tearing his sweatshirt at the seams.

He felt himself break free, out the front door. He sprinted into the night air, his legs carrying him faster than they ever had before. He ran in the dark, through the perfectly manicured lawns, his thoughts focused only on one thing.

He had to get far away, and he had to find somewhere to hide.

CHAPTER 22

Even though it was approaching eleven, the kid was still curled up in a ball on Tom's couch. A blue plaid quilt engulfed him like a cocoon and a pillow covered his head. Tom didn't have the heart to wake him; Trevor needed his sleep. It had been a rough night.

Tom's evening had gone much better, until the phone call. He and Carol had just returned from a nice dinner and a movie. Westwood Theatre was showing the classic 'Singing in the Rain' digitally re-mastered. He wasn't exactly sure what the technical jargon meant but the picture was incredible, and they both agreed it was almost worth the ten bucks a pop.

Then they went back to Tom's place and had some wine. Carol liked white zinfandel, which was actually pink—that just made no sense at all. He wasn't much of a wine drinker, but he was always willing to try new things for a special lady. They were getting cozy on the couch and then the phone rang.

"Mr.T! Thank God!" The kid sounded frantic, shouting into the phone. "You have to come get me! Please!"

"Trevor?"

"I'm in trouble—big trouble! Please I need your help."

What had the kid gotten himself into? "Okay kid, calm down. I can barely understand you. Slow down and tell me what's going on."

The kid finally took a breather and then whispered, "I'll explain everything later. I need you to come and get me Mr.T, like now."

A million questions were floating around in Tom's head, but his main concern was getting the kid out of there, wherever 'there' was. Tom could tell by the desperation in Trevor's voice, this was serious. He didn't waste any time, "Give me directions. I'll leave right away."

And so Tom and Carol's night was cut short. Instead of cuddling on the couch, they were cuddling in the front seat of his car as they drove out to Harbor Village.

Now Tom sat in his La-Z-Boy with a box of Ritz, looking over at the kid on the couch. He was sleeping peacefully, as if he had no worries in the world. He must be dog-tired. Trevor was not a restful sleeper.

Trevor had told him briefly about the party the night before. This kid couldn't catch a break. And it was lucky that Tom got there when he did, because if that Mr. Stewart character had found him, he probably would've cut the kid's balls off.

Trevor started tossing and turning, pulling the quilt up over his head and letting out a groan. *Back to reality*, thought Tom.

"Can I get you some coffee, kid? Water maybe?"

Trevor lifted the cover off his face and stared at Tom. He looked pitiful. His hair was all over the place and he had huge bags under his eyes. "No. Thanks," he mumbled.

Tom took a bite of his Ritz and waited. He still had a lot of questions, but he wasn't sure if now was the time.

"Mr.T, do you ever have the same dream over and over? Like not every night, but like you've had it ever since you can remember?"

Tom's thoughts immediately turned to Maddie. He had been having vivid dreams about her since her death. They weren't bad dreams necessarily. Most times she was just there—like an observer watching over him. But they were so real and it actually gave him comfort to see her.

"I guess maybe I have. I don't usually remember my dreams. Why do you ask?" Tom hoped the kid would open up. He had seen Trevor asleep enough times to know that nightmares were a common occurrence for him. He often screamed, and even thrashed out in his sleep.

"I have the same dream over and over." Trevor was staring up at the ceiling. "There is this man-in-black that chases me. Actually, I'm flying and I keep falling, like I can't stay up. He's on the ground waiting for me. I can see his face but I don't recognize him."

The kid stopped there and looked over at Tom. His voice started shaking, "Why does this stuff keep happening to me? Why can't I just get a break?"

Tom felt a rise of emotion swell up inside of him. He walked over to the couch and sat next to the kid. He put his hand on the kid's shoulder, "Trevor, you will get a break. I promise. Everyone is dealt a different hand in life. It's how we play the hand that matters."

He could see that this answer wasn't the one Trevor was looking for. Although he meant every word, it probably sounded cliché and trite.

The kid turned his back and buried his head into the pillow again.

Tom hated to see him like this, "Trevor, I want you to know something. You are an exceptional human being—a real diamond in the rough. I mean that sincerely."

At this, Trevor turned around. His cheeks were red and stained with tears, but he was smiling. "Thanks Mr.T. You're not so bad either."

The next thing he knew Tom felt the kid's arms wrap around him. Trevor squeezed him hard and held on to him like his life depended on it.

Maybe in the cruel world of Trevor McNulty, it actually did.

CHAPTER 23

One week later, Trevor was gazing into the aquarium at the Crazy Kids Center. Betty had found a new home in the hull of a sunken ship. The aquarium had recently been updated with a pirate theme, complete with mini treasure chests and skeletons. It fascinated Trevor like it would a three year old—maybe because these novelties weren't ever a part of his childhood.

The last week had been rough. He had called and texted Bea every day with no response. And when he called this morning, a recorded message came on saying the number was no longer in service.

He just wanted to tell her he was sorry one last time. But, she definitely never wanted to talk to him again, and Trevor couldn't blame her.

Mr.T suggested that Trevor go see Dr. Fisher and talk to her about everything. Of course Mr.T would say anything to get him to go back to the Crazy Kids Center.

At first Trevor laughed at the thought, but then he remembered his last session with Dr. Fisher. He still felt a little guilty about being such a jerk to her and in a weird way wanted to apologize somehow. What could it hurt?

The night of the party kept playing over and over in his head. The whole scene was still fresh in his mind: Evelyn falling on the floor, the wounded look on Bea's face and of course, Mr. Stewart trying to pulverize him.

But there was one thing that did give him some comfort. Lorene stuck up for him; she actually seemed to care about him. She probably risked her job making those excuses for him, and he just hoped she was still employed.

Trevor looked at his watch—3:58. He headed up to Dr. Fisher's office.

After a quick knock, she opened the door smiling, "Hello Trevor, come on in."

He took a seat in the 'patient' chair and she offered him something to drink, "I have coffee, tea, bottled water?"

He was tempted to give her his lecture on bottled water and its effect on the environment, but decided now probably wasn't the time. "Sure, I'll have some water."

She handed him the bottle of water and sat in her leather armchair, her notepad on her lap.

He took a long drink and looked down at the zigzag carpet, "First, I wanted to apologize to you. About our last session…I never should have talked to you that way."

"Trevor I accept your apology," she said simply.

"That's it?" This was much easier than he thought it'd be.

She smiled, "That's it. It's in the past. Let's move forward. So, how have you been?"

He took a deep breath, "Well it's been pretty insane actually."

At this Dr. Fisher sat forward, her hands clasped in front of her. "Tell me."

And so he told her. He told her about Bea, about Evelyn, and about the party. He told her pretty much everything that had happened since the morning in Harbor Village when he first met Bea.

She leaned back in her chair, "Wow, you *have* had a busy few weeks. How are you feeling about it all right now?"

He was exhausted. Just getting the story out took every ounce of effort he had. Although he had to admit, he did feel better for some reason. He felt a little lighter, less tense.

"I feel really tired—wiped out you know? I just wanted to get it off my chest."

"Yes, I know." There was something so calming about her voice, "I'm glad you told me about it."

He went on, "So do you have any advice for me—I mean, do you think Bea will ever talk to me again?"

"Well Trevor, I think you have to give her some time, and then see what happens. Giving her space is the only thing you can really do right now." It was the answer he pretty much expected.

He studied Dr. Fisher. She had it all—smarts, kindness and looks. He couldn't help himself. "You know, you're an attractive lady, smart and nice…." *God, he sounded like an idiot.*

"Thank you Trevor, but unlike Evelyn Stewart, I do prefer men out of high school," she smiled.

"No! That's not what I'm saying…I just wondered…" he could feel his cheeks flushing with embarrassment. "That guy in the lobby was married, right? Why would you be into a married guy? Just seems you could do a lot better."

Her smile faded, "Not that it's any of your business Trevor, but I am not romantically involved with that man you saw in the lobby."

"But you like him?" Why did Trevor care about this anyway? Why couldn't he just keep his mouth shut?

She sighed, "I did. But recently I realized how ridiculous the whole thing was. I broke it off—whatever *it* was."

Trevor knew he had probably gotten too personal. "I'm sorry, I should try to mind my own business."

"It's okay." Dr. Fisher began writing in her notebook, "The older you get, and the more life experiences you have, the more you realize that things aren't always as they seem."

She looked up, "Trevor, I have multiple sclerosis. Are you familiar with the disease?"

Whoa. His mind instantly filled with images of people in wheelchairs. He really didn't know much about it, but Dr. Fisher definitely didn't seem sick. He was confused, "Uh, no, not really. I mean I've heard of it."

She smiled, "Well, it's an auto-immune disease that affects the brain and central nervous system. I was diagnosed seven years ago when I was thirty. Strange things were happening inside my body and I just knew something wasn't right."

"What kind of things?"

She got out of her chair and walked over to the small window, "Oh, numbness, tingling—fun stuff like that. It's hard to describe to people, but it just felt like something wasn't right."

Trevor's curiosity instantly evaporated. He didn't want to hear any more, but now he was trapped inside the small office.

"At first, I thought maybe it was just nerves you know, maybe pre-wedding jitters."

Oh Shit. Wedding?

"They ran some tests and confirmed it was MS. Of course, I was devastated. I mean I was healthy—I ate healthy and exercised—did all the things you're supposed to do. You never expect a diagnosis like that."

Trevor had a feeling he knew what was coming next.

Dr. Fisher's voice was quiet, "I was with him for three years. Jeremy, my fiancé. We met in grad school.

The wedding was only four months away. Thank God the invitations hadn't gone out."

You just had to get personal, Trevor.

She turned to face him, looking surprisingly calm. "You know what is horrible? I actually thought about waiting until after the wedding to tell him. Just pretend I didn't find out until after. Isn't that sad?"

She was shaking her head, "But I told him right away and let him think about it. At first, Jeremy thought we should just postpone the wedding, and then as time went by... I guess down deep I knew the diagnosis would be a deal breaker for him. "

Couldn't keep your mouth shut, Trevor.

She walked back over to her chair and sat down, "And dating is difficult to say the least. You go on a couple of dates and then you have to worry about telling the person...I mean when should you tell? How do you say it?"

Trevor's therapy session had turned into Dr. Fisher's. She was actually looking at him like *he* might have the answers. He shrugged his shoulders; he had no clue how to react.

"It's so hard...I've pretty much given up on the whole dating scene. But, it gets lonely, and sometimes it's easier to get involved with people who have no expectations. Keep things simple, you know?"

She was smiling, but Trevor wasn't. He didn't know what the hell to say. "But, you seem so healthy. I would never know you had a disease like that."

"Like I said, things aren't always as they seem. I feel good most of the time. I get shots once a week and I take care of myself. In that respect, it hasn't changed my life greatly. It's the unknown—the future—that's hardest to face. It's too scary for some people."

She went on, "My work, and the patients I meet, keep me centered."

Trevor nodded, twiddling his fingers in his lap. He just hoped this talk was coming to an end. He felt like an even bigger bag of shit than he had when he walked into her office.

"Trevor, the reason I'm telling you this, besides the fact that if feels good to vent, is so maybe you can realize you are not alone. Sure, some people in this world often seem to have it made on the outside, but that usually isn't the case."

She paused, "And I'm not minimizing what has happened in your life. Please don't think that. I'm just hoping you can see that I have baggage too. If I can help you, it helps me. It's a win-win for both of us."

Just like Mr.T was always saying. *I do something for you. You do something for me. It goes both ways.*

Realization hit him hard. She had secrets. He had secrets. Everyone had secrets. And he wasn't sure why, but he trusted her completely. It was almost like they had their own private club; secrets were kept safe in this square office with the little window.

He could tell her things—things he hadn't told anyone. Not just about Bea and Evelyn and that whole mess. He could to tell her things about his past, about his mom…maybe even about *that* day.

She interrupted his thoughts, "Anyway, enough about all that. What do you think Trevor? Would you like to come back next week?"

He smiled, "Yea, I would like that."

When Trevor reached the door he turned around, "Hey, can I call you Dr. Fish?"

She chuckled, "Sure Trevor."

"Cool. See ya next week Dr. Fish."

CHAPTER 24

Trevor heard shouting and it sounded like Uncle Gary. He wondered what was up his ass. Trevor had been on Mr.T's couch all day watching Seinfeld re-runs. It was Sunday, and on this one day, Trevor could usually do what he wanted. He got up and walked over to the window facing the backyard.

The scene in front of him was like something out of a bad horror movie. A bare-chested Uncle Gary was holding up an axe, swinging it wildly through the air. His jeans were hanging low under his sagging gut, and his dirty white underwear stuck out by a good couple of inches. His bald head was blood-red and looked like it might explode at any minute.

Trevor's heart started pounding—this wasn't good. Maybe he was drunk. It wasn't typical on Sunday afternoons, but Uncle Gary was getting pretty extreme with his drinking lately. Whatever the reason, Trevor didn't have a good feeling about it.

"What's the racket?" Mr.T asked from the kitchen.

Before Trevor could answer, the scene went from bad to worse. Uncle Gary was heading for the Box.

"No!" Trevor yelled as he ran out the back door.

The maniac was going ballistic, screaming at the top of his lungs, "That son-of-a bitch! I'll kill the piss-ant!" Uncle Gary swung at the door of the Box. The lock split open with one shot.

Trevor ran through Mr.T's backyard, "Stop! Wait! Uncle Gary! Stop! Please!"

Uncle Gary stopped in the doorway and looked over at Trevor, his eyes wide with rage, "You piece of shit. I give you a roof over your head, and this is how you repay me?"

Confusion set in, mixed with panic. Trevor was at a loss, "What are you talking about?"

Uncle Gary leaned over, resting his hands on his knees, his hunched back heaving up and down. The out-of-shape bastard could barely catch his breath, but he never let go of the axe. "What am I talking about?!" He was shaking his head as he said it.

He looked up at Trevor with wild eyes, "Maybe you should ask Bill Stewart that question."

Trevor could feel his mouth go dry. His legs turned to jelly. "What do you mean, Bill Stewart? Did you talk to him?"

Uncle Gary stepped slowly toward Trevor, emphasizing every word as he said it, "Yes, I talked to him. And do you know what he told me, you shit-wad?"

As if on auto-pilot, Trevor could feel his feet back-peddling beneath him.

The maniac raged on, literally foaming at the mouth. "He told me that not only did you screw his daughter, but you went and fucked his old lady too!"

Trevor held his hands up in front of him, "Uncle Gary, it's not true...I swear..."

Just in time, Mr.T appeared at his side, "Now Gary, put the axe down. Let's talk about this—"

Before he could finish, Uncle Gary turned to Mr.T and began screaming, "You best shut up old man and mind your own damn business!

"And guess what else he told me?" His red face was turning an ugly shade of purple. "It seems Bill Stewart has a lot of friends in high places...even in shitty old Westwood. In fact, he has a friend on the Westwood City Council who owes him a favor."

Trevor did not like where this was going.

Then Uncle Gary laughed, a crazed, mad man laugh, "He is going to shut down McNulty Mechanics on some bullshit safety violations and there's not a thing I can do to stop him. My shop, my business, your grandfather's business—gone, just like that" He snapped his fingers in the air.

Before Trevor could fully digest what he had heard, Uncle Gary was stomping back over to the Box. "So, since you've taken everything away from me, I'm going to return the favor."

He disappeared inside and Trevor ran after him. "Uncle Gary! Please let me explain!" he pleaded.

When he entered the Box he saw Uncle Gary holding the axe high, positioned right over his work table. With one swoop the axe came down on the table, destroying the Windsor rocking chair Trevor had been working on. The axe came down again and again sending shards of wood flying everywhere. Trevor screamed for him to stop, but it was useless. In a matter of seconds, his work table was destroyed.

Without thinking, Trevor ran up behind him and grabbed around his fat neck. The hot, sweaty flesh was slippery beneath his arm and his uncle escaped easily. They stood across from each other like men in a boxing ring, waiting for the other to make a move.

Uncle Gary held the axe in front of him, panting as he said the words, "Don't you come any closer...or you'll be sorry!"

Trevor scanned the inside of the Box looking for something—anything—that would help him get the psycho out of there. As his mind raced and his adrenaline pumped, Trevor looked away for only a second, but that was all Uncle Gary needed. Something shiny flashed in the corner of Trevor's eye and then everything went black.

CHAPTER 25

Tom ran as fast as his boney old legs would allow. He had to get to a phone fast and call the police. That shit-for-brains had lost his mind and God only knows what he would do to Trevor.

This was one time Tom wished he had listened to the kid about getting a cell phone. Trevor always said it would be a good idea so they could get a hold of each other in case of an emergency. Well no doubt about it, this definitely qualified.

As he got back to his house, Tom found Jip jumping and barking at the back door. Poor little guy; he knew something was wrong.

Tom swung open the door and hurried over to the yellow rotary phone on the kitchen wall—another thing Trevor had poked fun at. "Really Mr.T? Not even push button?"

Tom's shaking fingers dialed the numbers, *911*.

"911, what is your emergency?"

"We need police right away! My neighbor is running around with an axe! He's trying to hurt a boy! Send someone quickly!" shouted Tom.

The woman on the other line was completely monotone, "Calm down sir…someone is on their way. Your address is 223 Greenview, is that correct?"

"Yes! Yes! Hurry please!" Tom pleaded.

"They are on their way. Sir, is anyone hurt?"

Tom stretched the chord on the phone as far as it would go so he could look out the back window. Trevor and Gary were still in the Box. God only knew what was happening inside. "I don't know! I have to go help him!"

"Sir, I need you to stay calm."

"Oh screw this." Tom dropped the phone and ran to the back door.

His heart sank. Gary was running from the Box, and a plume of black smoke followed him. *Oh no, God no.*

Moving faster than he had in years, Tom reached for a dish towel on the kitchen table. He turned on the sink and quickly soaked the towel in cold water. He threw open the back door, and hobbled out.

Tom was pushing his legs as hard as he could, but he felt like he was moving in slow motion. The smoke coming out of the Box was getting thicker; he could feel the heat as he got closer.

The kid was still in there. He had to get Trevor out!

When he approached the entrance, the heat was overwhelming. The black clouds of smoke were blinding; he couldn't see anything inside the Box.

Tom got down on his hands and knees and tied the dishtowel over his face. He blindly reached out onto the ground in front of him. As he began crawling into the Box, he instantly felt the searing heat on his skin. The acrid smell was overpowering and the sting in his eyes was excruciating.

He crawled further into the Box and breathing got more difficult. It felt like someone had wrapped a tight rubber band around his chest. *You've got to keep going Tom.*

Just then Tom felt something—an arm, and then a body. He squinted in the darkness and saw the outline of Trevor's face. He was out cold and bleeding badly from the head.

It was probably the adrenaline, but Tom felt a surge of strength that surprised him. He grabbed Trevor's arm and began pulling him toward the door. Everything in his body burned—his arms, his legs, his eyes, his lungs. *Tom, you have to get the kid out of here.*

Only a few feet separated them from the entrance, but he didn't know if he'd make it. He pushed his body to limits he had never taken it to before. *Just a little further…* Finally, he felt some patches of fresh air, and in a matter of seconds, they were outside.

Tom continued to pull the kid out into the grass, far away from the smoke and flames. When he couldn't go any further, he felt his body surrender.

Tom collapsed to his knees and fell on the grass next to Trevor. Ripping the towel from his face, he took in one last gulp of early summer air. He could hear sirens fading in the distance as he closed his eyes.

All of the pain seemed to melt away; his body felt light and his head clear. The feeling of peace was incredible. A brilliant light shined in the darkness and then Tom saw her—Maddie, as beautiful as the day he married her. She glowed like an angel, her smile radiant. She was waving him home.

CHAPTER 26

It had been a week since the big surprise party—the king-daddy of all surprise parties—and the Stewart house hadn't been the same. Mrs. Stewart took a vacation from her job and spent most days locked up in her bedroom with a bottle of Absolut. She had asked Lorene to move in full-time, to which Lorene politely declined.

Bill Stewart bought a condo in the city and Lorene hadn't seen him since. Good riddance. Appalled that she tried to cover for Trevor, he actually wanted to fire her. But Bea made such a fuss that he let it go. A divorce would probably come next, and as far as Lorene was concerned, it wouldn't be a bad thing.

Bea was a mess—just heart-broken. Things between her and Mrs. Stewart would never be the same. The girl had been hurt badly and Lorene didn't know if she would ever fully recover. Bea didn't understand why this was happening to her. She looked to Lorene for answers, but she simply didn't have them.

For three days after the party, Bea stayed in bed refusing to even come out of her room. Only because of Lorene's constant nagging, did she finally emerge from hiding.

And then the girl didn't speak, and barely touched her food. Lorene had tried making her favorites like chicken pot pie and spaghetti. Nothing worked—she picked at her food and sighed, and picked some more.

Today was no exception. Bea sat at the kitchen table with the usual sour puss face. She was twirling her fork back and forth through her linguini. She hadn't touched a bite.

Lorene put down the pot she was washing and walked over to the table. She sat across from Bea, and looked her straight in the eye. "Bea, now you have got to start eating something. A strong enough wind comes along, and you're going to blow right away!"

Not only had the girl lost weight, her face was pale, her eyes were puffy, and her hair actually looked greasy.

Bea barely glanced at her, "I'm not hungry Lorene."

She was at a loss. Maybe a little tough love was the way to go. "Bea, how do you think it makes me feel when I spend all that time making dinner for you, and you simply stare at it like a bump on a log? Every night it just goes to waste."

That got her attention, "I thought you took leftovers home to Reggie."

Maybe Lorene was finally getting somewhere. "I do, I do. But there are only so many left-overs my Reggie can eat! And besides, it makes me happy when *you* eat my food."

"Sorry" she said quietly. Now she had tears in her eyes.

Lorene put on her happy face, "Don't be sorry! Just eat, okay?"

Bea nodded.

Lorene thought it might be a good time to change the subject. "Hey, do you want to go shopping after dinner? We can go to the Gap, or that other store you love so much—the Coconut Republic" Lorene tried to sound serious. She hoped this goof would make Bea smile.

Bea looked up, and this time a slight grin was forming on her face, "You mean the Banana Republic, Lorene."

"Oh yea, of course...well, what do you say?"

Bea got up from the table. "Okay. Let me grab a sweatshirt." She ran upstairs.

Lorene felt an instant wave of relief wash over her. This was the first normal behavior she had seen from the girl in a week.

She picked up her purse and walked to the coat closet to grab her jacket. The evening news was playing on the flat screen, and as Lorene glanced at it, she stopped dead in her tracks.

In the center of the screen was a close-up of a face she knew all too well. The caption underneath read 'Teen Injured in Fire'. *Jesus Lord. It was Trevor.*

Lorene immediately ran over to the TV and turned down the volume. She didn't need Bea hearing this now. The reporter was standing in front of a small structure that was badly burned. *The Box!* The reporter then motioned to the garage, "Only a charred frame and piles of ash are what remains of this fire that injured seventeen year old Trevor McNulty."

Lorene picked up the remote to turn it off when Bea suddenly shouted from behind, "No! Don't Lorene! Oh my God! It's Trevor! Lorene, Trevor's hurt!"

Lorene immediately went to the girl and put her arms around her, "Now, calm down Bea. We don't know exactly what happened yet." She tried to listen to the tail-end of the report, but could only hear the last statement.

Apparently Trevor was at Southwest Hospital in serious condition. That was all she got. Lorene turned to Bea, "Okay, listen to me. I am going to call the hospital and see if I can get any more information."

Bea's eyes were wide, her voice shaking, "No Lorene! We are going to the hospital. I can't believe this. We have to make sure he's okay!"

Obviously it didn't matter how badly things had gone between the two kids. The girl still cared about Trevor.

"But Bea, honey…"

Bea was already half-way to the front door. "Whether you come or not, I'm going."

Lorene knew she wouldn't win this fight. The hospital probably wouldn't give her any information over the phone anyway. But there was no way she was letting Bea drive in her condition. The girl had a lead-foot as it was, and Lorene didn't need all of them ending up in the hospital. She sighed and grabbed her purse, "Okay, let's go."

***

"Are you family?" The young nurse at the desk asked. She was typing something into a computer and barely glanced up at them. She didn't look much older than Bea.

Lorene looked at Bea, "Uh…no. But we are like family to him. He really doesn't have any family in the truest sense of the word."

The nurse's hands stopped momentarily and she looked up, "Well I'm sorry but I can't give you any information unless you are immediate family. That is hospital policy."

Lorene had a feeling this was coming and she was afraid Bea might explode at any minute. This nurse would have to be swayed. She looked at the name tag on the nurse's crisp white shirt—Kristen Allen, RN.

"Look Kristen, may I call you Kristen? My…uh…friend here," she pointed to Bea, "was Trevor's girlfriend and they were very serious." A little fibbing couldn't hurt. "Could you just tell us something?

Anything? Please?" Bea's face was full of worry and very persuasive.

The nurse glanced around the station and then said quietly, "He suffered a head injury. The C-Scan showed a small skull fracture, but no brain injury, so that's good."

Lorene leaned in closer, "Wait—I heard on the news it was a fire."

"It was, but he was injured before the fire. He did suffer smoke inhalation and second degree burns on one of his arms too."

Bea interjected rather loudly, "Do you know how this happened?" The girl was losing her composure.

Nurse Kristen must've seen the desperation in Bea's eyes. Scanning the nurse's station once again, "Well I heard there was some kind of argument between Trevor and his uncle and his uncle set the garage on fire. Trevor was still inside. That's all I know, but it will probably be on the news."

Dear Lord.

The young nurse smiled at Bea reassuringly, "He should be okay though. If you come back in a couple days he'll probably be upgraded from serious condition. Then they allow non-family visitation and you could see him."

"Can't we see him now?" Bea pleaded.

"I'm really sorry. There's nothing I can do. He's probably under heavy sedation anyway."

Lorene smiled at Nurse Kristen and thanked her. They walked back toward the elevator and it wasn't long before Bea spoke her mind. "This is bullshit. He doesn't have immediate family."

Lorene knew the girl was frustrated, "There's nothing more we can do here Bea. I promise we'll come back as soon as we hear something."

They got into the elevator and the doors shut. Suddenly, Bea got wide-eyed, "Oh Lorene, what about Mr.Tyminski? Someone has to call him!"

Lorene hadn't thought about Tom. "I imagine he already knows what's going on. But you should probably call him anyway. He might be able to tell us more." She thought about the charred remains of the Box. If she remembered correctly, Tom and Trevor were neighbors. He must have witnessed some of this.

Bea pulled out her cell phone as they stepped off the elevator. "Yes, Westwood, Ohio. Yes, I need the number for Tom Tyminski—I believe on Greenview road...thanks." Bea bit her nails as she waited. Then she frowned at Lorene, "Ok, thanks." She clicked off her phone, "It's not listed."

Before Lorene could say anything, Bea stated matter-of-factly, "Well, we'll just go to his house. We can go right now, on our way home."

There was no point in arguing with the girl. "Okay…" Lorene sighed. She slipped her arm into Bea's, and they walked out into the parking garage together.

A bad feeling was creeping over Lorene, a feeling she just couldn't shake. Something told her there was more bad news to come—much more.

CHAPTER 27

Trevor opened his eyes to a mirage of blurry images. Waves of blue and green light passed in front of him; everything was out of focus. An unfamiliar voice with a British accent came from somewhere in the blur. "Trevor, can you hear me? Your eyes will need some time to adjust to the light. Give it some time."

Immediately a throbbing sensation began above his left eye. It felt like someone was stabbing him with a dull pencil. The ripple of pain shot through his head and forced him to close his eyes again.

The Brit continued, "You are in the hospital Trevor. You suffered some head trauma and it may take a little time for your vision to return to normal." He put something cold under Trevor's shirt causing him to flinch.

"I'm Dr. Novak. I'm a neurosurgeon at Southwest Hospital. Do you remember anything that happened Trevor?"

Of course he remembered. That asshole uncle of his destroyed the Box and came at him with an axe!

Trevor opened his mouth to speak, but his head hurt so bad, the words came out in a shriek, "Yes I remember. Jesus, can I get something for the pain?"

"We are administering the medicine now." The doctor's voice sounded farther away. "We want to bring you out of sedation occasionally to see how you're healing. Everything seems good so faarrrr…"

The words faded away from Trevor and a blanket of numbness settled over him. Pain-free and relaxed, he drifted into the nothingness once again.

***

Lorene and Bea drove from Tom Tyminski's house in silence. When they had gone to his home, there was no one there. They knocked and knocked, but got no answer. When they went around back to try the other door, they were faced with an awful scene.

Bright yellow crime tape circled the perimeter of Trevor' backyard. In the center, stood the Box that Trevor took such pride in—a black, crumbling pile of burnt wood and ash.

Underneath the rubble, Lorene could see metal tools that had managed to survive the flames. Perhaps some of those tools could be salvaged for the boy. She tried to think of something positive...the scene was just so horrible.

Of all the boys Bea could've gotten mixed up with, it had to be this one. It was pointless to try to talk her out of seeing him again. The girl had a mind of her own and would have to learn on her own. Lorene liked Trevor a lot, but the drama in this boy's life was more than most adults could handle, let alone a teenager.

Out of nowhere Bea yelled, "Turn there!"

The girl scared her half to death. "Bea! What are you yelling about? This isn't the way to the freeway."

Bea was pointing to a white sign on the side of the road, "There!"

As they got closer Lorene could read the black lettering, *Westwood Cemetery- est.1814*. The bad feeling that was sitting in the pit of Lorene's stomach suddenly grew times ten. Against her better judgment, she slowly pulled the car into the driveway leading to the cemetery.

Lorene was pretty sure she knew the answer but she asked anyway, "Now, what's this about? Why do you want to go *here* Bea?" Lorene wondered how much Bea knew about Trevor's mom. What exactly had he told her about his past and that horrible day?

Bea looked the same way Lorene felt—tired. She spoke in almost a whisper, "Trevor told me his mom is buried here. He told me a little bit about her, and I guess I just want to see."

Lorene sighed and continued down the drive. The cemetery was enormous—nothing but scattered grey stones over vast green hills that seemed to go on forever. How would they ever find the McNulty site?

Bea must have been thinking the same thing, "Maybe they have a caretaker or somebody we can ask."

Lorene scanned the cemetery and spotted a small brick building to the far right side. As they approached the building, Lorene noticed an old wood sign out front that had seen better days. Black, painted letters were chipped and faded in creepy cemetery fashion—OFFICE.

They parked the car and went inside. The small room was dimly lit and had a pungent musty odor. A reception desk sat on one side, and an array of stone samples lined the opposite wall. Church music played quietly in the background.

Lorene rang the silver bell on the desk and an elderly lady emerged from a room in the back. She was a tiny thing with patchy gray hair and glasses. Her back was hunched over so low, the edges of her pink cardigan almost touched the ground. She took careful baby steps toward them as they waited patiently.

"Hello. What can I do for you?" she creaked.

Lorene spoke loudly, "Hi. We were wondering if you could help us locate a grave."

The elderly woman suddenly fell back into the chair behind the desk.

"Oh! Are you okay?" Lorene asked.

The woman ignored her, and at a snail's pace reached into the desk drawer. "Sure, I can help you with that."

She opened up a large three-ring binder in front of her. "I'll just need a name and year of death."

Lorene glanced over at Bea who was on the other side of the room reading the gravestone samples. "Well, we aren't sure of the year exactly. It was a few years ago, 2010 I believe. The name would be McNulty, Paula McNulty."

The old woman abruptly stopped flipping through the pages and looked up at Lorene. She lowered her glasses and peered over them, her eyes so scrunched up, Lorene was sure they were closed, "*The* Paula McNulty?"

"Uh, yes. Paula McNulty." Lorene confirmed.

Without warning, the woman slammed the binder shut, making Lorene and Bea both flinch. "Well, I know that one. Kind of infamous around here you know." She rattled it off eerily, "It's section twenty-three, row fourteen, grave six."

She continued, "You drive straight back to the large angel monument on your right. If you walk due east from there to the middle of that section, you'll find it. There are metal markers in the ground next to all of the sites with numbers on them. The number you want is 23146." She scribbled it on a post-it note and handed it to Lorene.

"Thank you very much," Lorene took the note and grabbed Bea's arm. "C'mon, let's go." She just wanted to get this over with.

They got in the car and slowly drove to the angel monument. Following the old woman's directions, they walked east to the middle of the section, scanning the names on the gravestones as they went.

"Bea honey, I have to ask why you want to do this. What do you hope to gain from visiting his mom's grave?"

Bea was a couple of rows over. "I don't know Lorene...I just want to see it, okay? I'm not sure why. Maybe because it's a part of his past. I'm just trying to understand all of this, you know. I..." She stopped mid-sentence.

Bea was now on her knees reading the stone in front of her. "I found it!"

Lorene stepped carefully through the maze of gravesites and stood behind Bea. She read the small stone in front of her:

PAULA MCNULTY
February 2, 1974 – September 21, 2010

"Oh my God..." Bea whispered.

Lorene knelt down beside Bea and put her arm around the girl. Chills went up her spine.

Bea's voice was shaking as she pointed to the smaller stones in front and read the names:

ALLISON MCNULTY   *JACOB MCNULTY*
2007 – 2010   *2004 – 2010*

Lorene already knew the tragic story of Trevor's past from researching it. But seeing these children's tiny graves was almost more than she could bear.

"What's going on? I don't understand this."

Lorene could feel tears welling up in her eyes. The day had been an emotional roller coaster from the start. "I wasn't sure about what he had told you, or even if it was my place to tell you. I thought maybe you'd look it up online. You were thirteen when it happened so I'm sure you weren't keeping up on the latest news…"

"Wait! News? Lorene, what are you talking about!?"

"Then you two broke up…I guess I should've told you the whole story before this."

Bea looked more confused than ever; she wanted answers. Lorene let out an exhausted sigh, "I'm not really sure where to begin. Let's go sit over there."

A small stone bench stood appropriately under a weeping willow. They sat down and Lorene began telling the story.

CHAPTER 28

Another unfamiliar voice was calling his name. "Trevor! Trevor! Can you hear me?"

He opened his eyes to blurry images which slowly came into focus. A short smiling Asian man was standing over him.

"Trevor, hello!" he said in a thick Chinese accent. "I am your nurse today. My name is Kym." He pointed to a large whiteboard on the wall across from his bed. Giant red letters spelled out, 'KYM Day Nurse'.

Kym continued talking very loudly with the same stupid smile plastered to his face. He was not helping Trevor's pounding head one bit. "There is a man here to see you. Do you feel like you can talk?"

Anything would be better than listening to more of Kym. "Yeah, I guess." His throat was killing him. "Can I have some water though?"

"Sure, sure, of course." Kym reached over to the pink plastic water pitcher and poured him a cup. He held it to Trevor's lips while he drank. His mouth was so dry; it felt like his tongue was velcroed to the roof of his mouth. As the cold liquid went down his throat, it filled all of the parched cracks and crevices. It was the best water he had ever tasted.

As he finished his drink, a tall African-American man walked in. He was probably in his fifties, completely bald, and well-dressed. He also had a very serious expression on his face.

Nurse Kym scurried out of the room. Uneasiness crept into the pit of Trevor's stomach.

The man walked over to the side of Trevor's bed and sat in the chair, "Hello Trevor, I'm Detective Mike Walker from the Westwood Police Department." He pulled out a badge from his inside coat pocket and flipped it open.

Trevor barely glanced at it. "Hi," his voice creaked—God, he sounded pathetic.

"How are you feeling son?"

There was something about the word 'son' that made him feel a little more at ease, and Trevor felt his insides relax a bit. "Truthfully, not so great."

The detective leaned in closer, "And I'm really sorry about that, but time is of the essence." He paused and looked over at Nurse Kym who had re-entered the room. Kym was standing on the side of the bed fluffing the same pillow over and over. "Do you think we could have a word in private?" the detective asked.

Kym's permanent smile suddenly faded, "Oh, sure." He looked directly at Trevor, "If you need anything—anything at all—you just push that button. Okay?"

Detective Walker turned his attention back to Trevor, "Son, do you think you can answer some questions for me?"

The throbbing in his head was getting worse. "Yeah, I guess."

The detective pulled out a pad and pen and Trevor suddenly felt like he was in some bad movie drama—the whole thing was just surreal. "What do you remember about the events of last Sunday when..." he pointed to Trevor's head, "this happened?"

He may have suffered head trauma, but it definitely hadn't affected Trevor's memory of that day. The scene was crystal clear in his mind and he slowly began telling the detective everything: Uncle Gary swinging his axe like a madman, the look in his eyes, the confrontation in the Box—all of it. "He must've hit me with the axe. I don't remember anything after that—just waking up here."

Detective Walker was jotting down notes in his pad, "You were fortunate he got you with the blunt end."

"Yea, real fortunate."

"Do you have any idea where your uncle may have gone?"

Trevor's stomach turned, "You don't know where he is? Seriously? Jesus, he could be anywhere—I have no idea." Then a thought suddenly came to Trevor, "But, Mr.T was there... maybe he saw something. Did you talk to him? And my dog Jip! Is Mr.T taking care of him?"

The detective looked down at his pad of paper, "Your dog is fine. A woman named Carol Sorak is taking care of him. She said she was a friend of yours." He paused, "By Mr.T, I assume you are referring to Tom Tyminski?"

"Yeah, old guy... he lives next door to me, a good friend of mine. He was right there. He probably saw the whole thing."

The detective sighed, "Trevor, I'm sorry to tell you this, but Tom Tyminski was pronounced dead at the scene."

As the words were spoken, Trevor felt his face grow numb, then his fingers, and then his whole body. The words faded into the background—he wasn't hearing them right. He didn't say...

Trevor desperately searched the detective's face, "This can't be right. No, no, Mr.T was outside—he was never in the Box with us. He wasn't there! This has to be a mistake!"

Detective Walker's expression didn't change. "I'm sorry son. Tom Tyminski died on scene from a heart attack—probably brought on by smoke inhalation."

Smoke inhalation? "I...I don't get this! Smoke inhalation? There wasn't a damn fire!" Trevor's head was spinning. This couldn't be happening. "Where was the fucking fire?" he felt his voice cracking.

Just then Nurse Kym entered the room, "Okay Trevor, the monitors are telling me your blood pressure is going up." He walked over to the IV machine and hung a new bag adjusting one of the plastic tubes. "I think we need to cut the chat short guys, okay?"

Detective Mike nodded and started to get up. Trevor grabbed his arm, "No! Please don't go yet. First you need to tell me how this happened!" Maybe the detective was wrong, maybe he had the wrong guy, maybe Mr.T was okay...*Mr.T had to be okay.*

The detective looked over at nurse Kym who simply said, "Five minutes," and then walked out of the room.

"We have a few witnesses—neighbors who were having a cookout a couple of houses down. They saw the whole thing, and from what we can gather, after your argument, your uncle apparently set the garage on fire. You were unconscious inside—struck by a blunt object, probably the axe."

"The Box..." Trevor whispered to himself.

The detective paused, "When the neighbors saw the smoke, they ran over and that's when they saw Tom Tyminski pulling you out of the fire. Another minute or two probably would've been too late. He saved your life."

Trevor let the words sink in. Mr.T had saved his life. The old man had pulled him out of the burning garage and it had killed him.

The feelings inside him were too overwhelming and he felt himself floating toward the numbness once again. Everything got blurry, and then once again, went black.

CHAPTER 29

"You almost ready Bea?" Lorene shouted up the stairs.

Four days had passed since that awful day when they visited the cemetery. They were going to try to visit Trevor in the hospital again. Lorene was able to get some details on how he was doing, now that he was upgraded to fair condition. Apparently he was awake and talking, but still healing from his head wound. As a precaution, he wouldn't be released for another day or two.

Lorene was truthfully a little worried about visiting the boy. She wasn't sure how he would react to seeing Bea, and she didn't want to upset him in any way.

Not long after they left the cemetery, Lorene learned of Tom Tyminski's passing from watching the evening news. Lorene hadn't known Tom very long, but the news was still crushing. He seemed like such a lovely man, and was obviously important to Trevor. The funeral would be held tomorrow and Lorene assumed Trevor wouldn't be able to attend, which was heartbreaking as well.

So many thoughts raced through her head as she waited for Bea. She wondered where the boy would go. Tom Tyminski was all he had and Trevor would be turning eighteen soon. Would he drop out of school or live on the streets?

Lorene decided she would just have to help Trevor in any way she could. She could only hope that this loss wouldn't be the final straw for him. There was only so much a boy could take!

Bea came down the stairs slowly, "I'm ready."

The girl seemed visibly upset about something, "You okay Bea?"

"Yes, I'm fine," she said.

But Bea didn't seem fine. Lorene knew her too well, and something was definitely bothering her. She had been crying. "Are you nervous about seeing Trevor?"

She sighed, "No, I guess I just realized something."

"What's that hon?" Lorene asked.

Bea shook her head, "It's nothing, really. Let's just go."

The girl obviously wasn't in the mood for talking about it, "Okay." Lorene grabbed her purse and they were out the door.

***

When Trevor woke up this time, his stomach lurched immediately as he remembered what the detective had told him earlier. *Mr. Tyminski was dead because of him.* Trevor put his head back down on the pillow and stared at the ceiling. Tears streamed out of the corners of his eyes.

He just couldn't take anymore. He was done—done with everything. His life had been nothing but shit. Every time he thought things might start going his way, he was shoved back to square one.

He had always tried to do the right thing, even when he thought everything was lost. When all he saw was darkness, he found his way out. He had the idea for the Box, and then for the Haven House. He felt good about what he was doing. Now it was gone—all of it.

He also had lost the only girl he ever really cared about. Bea hated him—that was obvious. She was the one friend he had, other than Mr. T...and now they were both gone.

Why? Why him? Was he cursed? Was it just bad luck, or maybe Karma? Or was this all some big test? How much more could he handle before breaking?

No, he was already broken. Broken badly.

Just then Nurse Kym entered the room carrying a tray with some brown plastic bowls on it. "Hello, sleepy head. How are you feeling today?"

Trevor turned his head to the opposite side and stared out the window. It was sunny today, nothing but blue skies.

Completely ignoring Trevor's silent treatment, Kym continued, "Well the doctors have put you on a new diet. You are allowed to have solids now. Yay!"

Trevor looked back at Kym with his ridiculous smile. He was actually wearing a smock with Tweety Birds all over it. Was this guy for real?

"I'm not really hungry." He closed his eyes again.

Nurse Kym pulled the rolling table over to the bed. He slid it over Trevor's body until the tray of food was hovering directly over his chest. An overwhelming stench of beef broth found its way up to his face, and he thought he might puke right there.

With every ounce of strength he had, Trevor pushed the table away and pulled himself up as far as he could. "I told you I'm not hungry! And I'm also a vegetarian by the way. Get that shit out of here—it's making me sicker!"

Nurse Kym actually frowned, "Okay, okay. I'm taking it away!" He held his hands up in surrender and grabbed the tray. "I'll go see what else they have. Geez!"

Trevor turned toward the window when he heard footsteps entering again. "Back already?" he called over his shoulder.

"Hi Trevor."

His heart jumped; it was Bea. He slowly turned back to face her. She was standing next to his bed with her hands clasped in front of her, and she was smiling. Could she have had a change of heart? Maybe they had a chance after all.

Her hair was different. It was light brown now and longer than before. "Hey, did you do something to your hair?" *God, what a lame thing to say.*

She tucked a strand of her hair behind one ear, "Yeah, I lightened it. Time for a change I guess…" Her words trailed off.

"Well, it looks really good." Trevor's mind raced as he thought of what to say next. He had nothing to lose at this point, and he might not get another chance.

He closed his eyes, because for some reason it was easier that way. "Bea I am so sorry about everything. I mean, I'm not sure how all of this stuff got so messed up with your mom… and I just want you to know that what she said that happened between us—it wasn't true. I swear it never happened."

"It's okay Trevor," she interrupted. "You don't have to explain. My mom's got major issues. I'm just sorry she got you involved in her crap."

He opened his eyes slowly. Why was it so hard to look at her?

She sat down on the bed next to him. She looked calm and relaxed and that put him a little more at ease. She grabbed his hand, "I wanted to tell you I was so sorry to hear about Mr. Tyminski."

At the mention of his name, Trevor felt his heart sink again. He felt the tears welling up and he focused his eyes on the ceiling. He didn't want to break down in front of her.

"Trevor I also wanted to tell you—."

Without thinking, he reached up and pulled her close, until they were staring into each other's eyes, "Let's just start over, okay?" He leaned in and kissed her gently. He missed her soft lips, her warm skin, and her comforting touch.

"Stop," she pulled away from him. "Trevor, I came here to tell you that I care about you, and I'm so sorry about what's happened…and I'm so sorry about Mr.T. But I still can't be with you in that way. I just can't."

He was confused. She was being really nice, and it was giving him mixed signals.

She went on, "You've been through a lot in your life and I want you to know I will always be there for you as a friend. I had to tell you that."

Trevor was at a loss for words. *Friends?*

She wasn't finished, "I'll be going to college next year, and you'll be doing something great, whatever that is. I sincerely hope we can stay in touch."

Bea squeezed his hand, but he had nothing to say. Maybe it was the drugs they were giving him, but Trevor couldn't speak. He felt completely numb. Everything in his life had pretty much turned to shit, and this just added to the pile.

CHAPTER 30

The coffee in the hospital cafeteria smelled better than it tasted. But the cinnamon danish was pretty good. It had been at least half an hour since Bea had gone in to visit Trevor. Lorene decided it was probably safe to head up to his room now.

While walking in the hallway, she met a very bubbly nurse named Kym. When she asked at the desk for Trevor's room, he came running over and introduced himself. He was very eager to inform Lorene all about Trevor's condition and to assure her he was being well taken care of. Oh Lord! She could only imagine what Trevor thought of Nurse Kym. He was a hoot!

"Knock, knock!" She tapped lightly on the open door, but got no answer. She walked into the room and found Trevor alone. Bea was nowhere to be found.

"Hello Trevor." As Lorene got closer, she stopped in her tracks.

My Lord, he looked horrible. The side of his head was wrapped in gauze like he had just returned from the battlefield. And he looked so thin! Trevor was already a skinny thing, but in that short time he had withered away to almost nothing.

Lorene tried to hide her surprise and attempted a meager smile. "How are you feeling Trevor?" She asked cautiously.

"Good to see you Lorene," his voice was pitiful.

She looked around the room, "Uh, I thought maybe Bea would be here."

"She was, but I think she went looking for you." Trevor sighed, "In case you're wondering, Bea told me she just wants to be friends."

"I see." Even with all the drama, this was still a little bit of a surprise to Lorene.

"Lorene I wanted to thank you for trying to cover for me at the party. Even though it didn't quite work out…"

"Well I'm just sorry you had to deal with Mrs. Stewart. I've worked for that woman for a long time and she has some issues she needs to work out. She's quite a troubled woman, and I'm sorry you had to get mixed up in everything."

Lorene didn't want to upset the boy further, but she had to offer her condolences, "Trevor, I was so sad to hear about Mr.Tyminski. I didn't know him well, but I could tell he was a very good soul. I'm so sorry."

Lorene sat down in the vinyl chair beside his bed. "I wanted to let you know that the funeral is tomorrow."

Trevor's eyes closed, "You know, it doesn't seem real. I almost don't believe it, I mean, they just tell me Mr.T is…not here anymore…and expect me to just accept it. Well I can't."

Lorene paused as thoughts swirled around in her head. "I know you obviously can't make the funeral, but I will definitely say a prayer for you."

"Thanks. I'll say goodbye in my own way when I get out of here."

Trevor would probably be discharged in a couple of days, and Lorene wanted to talk to him about where he would go when he was released.

She studied the boy in front of her. He was so fragile. Should she even be making this offer right now? Maybe this just wasn't a good time. Then again, maybe there never would be a good time.

"Trevor, I know you probably haven't given it much thought, but I wanted to throw it out there. My husband Reggie and I would love it if you would come and stay with us."

She watched his face, but he showed no reaction, "Just until you can get back on your feet. You'll be turning eighteen soon and I know you can legally be on your own, but I thought maybe you could use the company." She was rambling, "My kids are grown and in college…"

The boy simply stared ahead. Maybe this wasn't such a good idea.

"And Reggie and I just thought…well maybe it could do all of us some good." She searched his face for something, anything.

Trevor suddenly reached over, grabbed her hand, and squeezed it tight. Then to her surprise, he attempted a smile, "Sure, I'd like to come stay with you Lorene. I'd like that a lot."

CHAPTER 31

He was flying again—over the open fields and barren trees. The man-in-black was below him, slashing his arms through the air, trying to catch him. Trevor was falling lower and lower, closer to his grasp. He couldn't keep this up much longer! The man caught his leg and in one swift motion, pulled him down to the ground with a thud. The man was on top of him, and Trevor could see his face clearly.

"Trevor, can you hear me?" the man asked.

He opened his eyes, but the face was still there. He blinked again—still there. Trevor was awake, and the man hovering over his hospital bed was the man-in-black! *No!*

Panic set in and he let out a frightened yell, "What the hell!? Stay away from me!" He sat up in bed and pulled the covers up, like somehow that was going to protect him. "Get away from me."

"Whoa, kid, calm down." The man looked surprised. "I think you were having a bad dream. I'm not going to hurt you or anything. I'm just here to ask you some questions."

Trevor desperately scanned the rest of the room. It was empty; they were all alone. Suddenly, it felt like someone had turned up the thermostat to a hundred degrees. He started sweating and was finding it hard to breathe. The nurse call button! He grabbed it and started pushing it rapidly.

The man-in-black stared at Trevor as though he were crazy, like he had suffered some serious brain damage. Maybe he had. Maybe he was just seeing things. Or, maybe he was still in his dream—one of those dreams inside a dream.

A nurse he had never seen before entered the room. She had to be pushing three hundred pounds and had some major hair-lip going on.

"Can I help you with something?" she sighed, like it wasn't her job. Nurse Kym was looking pretty good right now.

The words flew out of Trevor's mouth in a frantic plea, "Please, can you make him leave?" He pointed to the man-in-black.

Looking thoroughly bothered, Nurse Ratchet walked over to Trevor and handed him a little paper cup. Inside were three pills that almost looked like candy. One was yellow, one was pink, and one was blue. He could swear the blue one had a smiley face on it. "It's time for you to take your pills. Let's calm down, okay."

Her attitude was as ugly as her face. Trevor felt rage rising up inside of him. He couldn't take this bed anymore, these nurses, or this frickin hospital for that matter. "Don't patronize me! I don't give a shit about the damn pills. I want him out of here!" he shouted. "Now!"

Nurse Ratchet's eyes grew wide and she took a step back.

"Trevor!" The man-in-black yelled. He looked pissed, "I don't know what the deal is, but I am just here to ask you some questions." He paused and reached into his jacket. *Jesus, was he pulling out a gun?*

Relief flooded Trevor as he realized it was just a wallet. *Get a grip Trevor!*

The man took a step forward and flipped it open. A shiny silver badge and some kind of ID were inside. "My name is Brian O'Donnell. I'm the chief arson investigator with the Cleveland Police Department."

Trevor was more confused than ever. *The man-in-black was an arson investigator?*

"Yes, I'm an arson investigator." The man said impatiently, as if reading Trevor's mind.

None of this made any sense, "Okay... so what do you want to ask me? I already talked to the detective."

The investigator pulled up a chair next to his bed. "Can I sit?"

Knowing the man wasn't going to kill him or anything, Trevor relaxed a bit and nodded.

Investigator O'Donnell continued, "Its standard procedure when there is any type of fire, especially if foul-play is suspected. We have to determine if the fire was arson and if so, who's responsible? Again, this is just procedure for the investigation—to put it on record."

Trevor shrugged his shoulders, "Fire away…no pun intended."

O'Donnell didn't appear amused. "Can you tell me your account of what happened last Sunday afternoon at your residence?"

And so Trevor began retelling the story of that Sunday afternoon. The short and not-so-sweet version which went something like: Uncle Gary went crazy, hit him over the head, burned down the box, and tried to kill him. And no, he had no idea where the asshole was hiding.

O'Donnell seemed to be listening intently, but unlike detective Walker, he hadn't written down a thing. He just watched Trevor. He was probably one of those experts on body language or something. "Aren't you going to write anything down?" Trevor asked.

"No need. We pretty much know how this went down. I'm sure the detective told you, some of your neighbors saw the whole thing. It all corroborates with your story. Once we find your uncle he'll be facing a slew of serious charges, arson being just one of them." O'Donnell stood up from his chair and turned to leave. "If we need anything else, I'll be in touch."

"Wait!" Trevor couldn't let him just walk away. The guy already thought he was a freak, so it couldn't hurt to ask. "Have we met somewhere before? You seem very familiar to me."

O'Donnell walked back to the chair and sat down. "I guessed by your reaction when you woke up, that you must've remembered me."

Remembered from where?! Trevor's mind was racing. This man was in his nightmares and had haunted him for years, but he honestly didn't know why. "No. I don't remember you."

The man-in-black leaned back in his chair and said simply. "I was the investigator on your mother's case."

CHAPTER 32

It had been almost a week in the hospital when the doctors finally decided to let him go. And two days had passed since his visit from Investigator O'Donnell, aka, the man-in-black. If it wasn't for the visits from Lorene, he might have lost his mind. She kept him occupied with her small talk and kept his thoughts away from the fire— from both fires.

Trevor had nothing to take with him but the clothes on his back, which Lorene had been nice enough to buy. They were just t-shirts and jeans, but still nicer than anything he had ever owned. She had offered to pick him up too, but he told her he had some things to take care of. Luckily, she didn't ask any questions. He still planned on staying with Lorene, but there was someone else he had to see first.

As Trevor stepped out of the revolving door of the hospital lobby, he turned his head up to the sun and let the warmth wash over his face. The winters may suck in Cleveland, but the summers weren't so bad—warm and breezy with bright blue skies.

He did his best to empty his mind, as he had done repeatedly since the man-in-black left his room two days ago. Trevor knew if he could just hold it together until he got out of the hospital, he might be able to find a way to deal with everything. *Might.*

The sound of a honking horn jarred him out of his semi-meditative state. A silver sedan pulled up alongside the curb with a blond woman in the driver's seat. His ride.

He walked over to the passenger side and leaned into the open window. "Thanks a lot for coming."

She smiled and said, "No problem, get in." Trevor opened the door and got in.

***

Lorene had just finished polishing the last of the silver flatware when the doorbell rang. In the quiet house she jumped at the sound. For a change, Mrs. Stewart was out somewhere and Bea was at the beach.

The girl improved a little bit every day. She got a summer job at the mall and started going out with her girlfriends. Although she had decided to end things with Trevor once and for all, it didn't seem to bring her down.

Lorene was still surprised at how strong the girl appeared. One day she seemed desperate and determined to work things out with Trevor. But a couple of days later, she was telling him she just wanted to be friends. Maybe learning about his horrific past was just too much to handle.

Lorene went to the door humming an old Donna Summer tune. Listening to the oldies station always seemed to make the work go a little faster.

She opened the door to find a pretty brunette woman standing in front of her. She had kind eyes and a warm smile—probably in her forties if Lorene had to guess. Her hair was cut short into one of those angled bobs and she was very sharply dressed in a crisp white blouse and navy slacks. Lorene had done enough of the Stewart's dry cleaning to recognize expensive clothes when she saw them.

"Hello. Can I help you?" Lorene asked in her most professional housekeeper voice.

The woman hesitated for a second and then extended her hand, "Hello. My name is Jean Tyminski."

Lorene felt sympathy wash over her as she realized who the woman was. They shook hands. "Tom Tyminski was my father."

"Of course, of course... Please do come in!" Lorene motioned the woman into the foyer. "I'm Lorene, the family housekeeper. I was so sorry to hear about your father. I met him only briefly but he seemed like a wonderful man."

"Thank you. He was wonderful—the best father a daughter could ever ask for."

Lorene could see the pain in her eyes. "Well come have a seat. I can make us some tea." She made her way to the sink to fill the teapot.

Jean Tyminski sat at the kitchen table, "I don't want to take up a lot of your time. I was hoping you might know where I could find Trevor McNulty?"

Lorene had guessed as much when she heard the woman's last name. It was the only reason Lorene could think of as to why she was there.

Jean continued, "I called the hospital and they told me he was released. They wouldn't give me any more information, so I went down there myself. I found one of the nurses who took care of him and he reluctantly gave me your name. He told me you had visited with another friend of Trevor's, a young girl named Bea Stewart?"

Lorene smiled, "Yes, Bea is a good friend of Trevor's."

"Well, I'm sorry about bothering you like this. I found this address online and I just didn't know where else to go. I am only in town for a couple of days and I really wanted to speak to Trevor. I was hoping to see him at the funeral, but I'm guessing he couldn't make it."

Lorene raised her hands up, "It's no problem at all. Bea and I were at the funeral, and now I remember seeing you there. Trevor very badly wanted to go but he just wasn't well enough. I'm sure it broke his heart not to be there."

"I'm sure it did." Jean smiled again. "My father talked about Trevor often. He was like a grandson to my father. I would very much like to meet him before I head back to California."

"Of course. Just so you know, he has agreed to come stay with me temporarily until he gets things figured out. So I'm sure I'll be seeing him later today."

"Oh good," Jean began digging in her purse. "Thank you so much. I'll give you my cell phone number and you can call me. Or if Trevor wants to call me himself, that's fine too." She handed the slip of paper to Lorene.

"We'll do," Lorene showed her to the foyer. "It was so nice to meet you Jean. I will definitely be in touch."

Jean nodded and headed out the front door. As she walked down the brick pathway, Lorene's thoughts turned to Tom Tyminski. He must've been a special man; it was obvious his daughter loved him very much.

And it was obvious that Trevor loved him very much as well. In the midst of their terrible loss, maybe the two of them could find some comfort in each other.

CHAPTER 33

"I'm glad you called me. How are you feeling?" Dr. Fisher closed the office door behind her. She sat across from him and picked up a yellow pad from the side table placing it on her lap.

"Do you mind not taking any notes...I need to get this out. Can you just listen?" Trevor knew he sounded like a desperate ass, but he didn't care. He just needed to start talking; just let it out now.

"Sorry, bad habit." She put the pad on the side table.

He looked over at the window. Nothing but blue. *Talk Trevor.* "I never told you about my nightmares—about the man-in-black?"

She shook her head, "We didn't get that far."

"Well, I've had these dreams for as long as I can remember. They are always pretty much the same. I'm flying over this open field and there's this man on the ground chasing me. He's wearing all black. I keep falling toward the ground and I know he's trying to catch me…"

"Does he ever catch you?" she interjected.

"Sometimes, and then I usually just wake up." His head felt so heavy; he was exhausted. "Well I figured out who he is. He's an arson investigator."

Trevor looked down and concentrated on the zigzag pattern in the carpet. "He came to the hospital to see me. I recognized him right away as the man in my nightmares, but I couldn't remember where I had seen him before."

He felt a huge lump forming in his throat. "He wanted to ask me some questions about the fire at the Box." He felt like he might choke on his own words, "And then he told me."

"Go on Trevor."

Tears began dripping from his cheeks and falling into his lap. "He told me that he was there."

Dr. Fisher reached over and handed him a tissue, "Where Trevor? Where was he?"

He looked up at her, "Four years ago."

The empathetic gaze on Dr. Fisher's face changed before him. He could see a spark of realization in her eyes. She spoke softly and asked him the one question he never thought he'd be able to answer, until now. "Trevor," she said, "Can you tell me what happened four years ago?"

His heart was racing and his head was pounding. He took a deep breath and tried to calm himself. He couldn't keep it bottled up any longer. "I think I need to go back further. I think I should start at the beginning—at least the beginning that I remember."

***

Trevor woke up to screaming.

Mom was really mad this time—shouting louder than he had ever heard before.

"That bastard! His soul mate? His fucking soul mate?! He leaves me with two mouths to feed! A fucking baby to take care of!"

Jacob, Trevor's little brother, wasn't even a year old yet. He was screaming too, but Mom ignored him. After a few minutes, things finally got quiet and Trevor felt like it was safe to come out of his bedroom.

He walked out into the small living room and found Mom sitting on the couch with a piece of paper in her hands. He walked over to her slowly; he wanted to hug her and tell her it would be okay.

Mom looked different, her eyes looked crazy. "Do you know what this is Trevor? It's a note from your father. You can read now, can't you? Here!" She forced the paper into his hands and screamed, "Read it!"

Why was she angry with him? He didn't do anything. The tears filled his eyes, but he tried to hold them back. Mom didn't like it when he cried—she said she had enough crying with the baby.

The black writing on the yellow paper looked like scribble to him. He was only seven and didn't know how to read cursive yet. "What's it say, Mama?" he whispered, trying to hide the fear in his voice.

She shook her head, "You don't just look like him— you're an idiot like him too!" She ripped the note out of his hands.

Now she began talking in her quiet, calm voice. That was the voice that scared Trevor the most. "What it says is that your father has left us. He has found his fucking soul mate and is never coming back. That is what it says."

Trevor felt sadness and anger set in. It couldn't be true. How could Dad do this to him? How could he leave him and Jacob with Mom?

Dad wasn't around that much, but when he was home, he was nice to Trevor. Sometimes Dad even bought him gum or Pokémon cards. Dad never smacked him, or called him mean names like Mom did.

"I'm so sorry Mama." He walked toward her and tried to hug her.

She put her hands up in front of him and stopped him. "No Trevor. Not now." She crumpled the note into a ball and threw it across the room. "Go back to bed Trevor." She walked away, into her bedroom, still ignoring Jacob who had cried himself to sleep.

***

"Trevor, do you want to take a breather?" Dr. Fisher asked.

"No. I want to keep talking if that's okay."

Dr. Fisher walked over to a mini-fridge on the corner of her desk. "Would you like one?" She was holding out a bottle of Dasani. She smiled, "It's important to stay hydrated."

"Sure." Trevor took a long drink of the bottled water. His throat was dry from all of the talking, and it tasted good. He would lecture her about the bottles another day.

Dr. Fisher sat back down across from him. "So was this about the time your mom started her phobic behavior with the kleenex?"

"No that came later. She just started hiding in her bedroom a lot—like most of the day. I mean, she got me up for school in the morning. She would get me a bowl of cereal and make my lunch, you know help me get to the bus... But, then she started going out at night and sleeping in. I started missing a lot of school."

He took another sip of water, "So, she bought me an alarm clock and showed me how to use it. She also showed me how to get my cereal, make a peanut butter and jelly sandwich, and how to do laundry."

"Trevor, what grade were you in, do you remember?"

"I don't know—like first, second maybe?"

Dr. Fisher nodded, "That's a lot of responsibility for a first grader."

Trevor shrugged his shoulders, "Well, she did have to take care of Jacob. She would always say to me 'Trevor, I get no sleep taking care of a baby. I am exhausted and I need my sleep when I can get it. I need you to be a big boy and get yourself ready in the morning.' So, that's what I did."

"Did she ask you to help take care of your brother?"

"Not yet." He went on, "She kept Jacob in the bedroom with her. He seemed fine until that one day…"

"What day?"

Trevor felt his eyelid begin to twitch, "The day I came home from school and he was screaming."

His hands instantly became wet with sweat and he wiped them on the front of his jeans. "It was such a weird scream, not like his normal cry. I ran back to Mom's bedroom and found him lying in his crib. His face was all red, and when I picked him up, I noticed his diaper was soaking wet. I looked over at the bed, but mom wasn't there. Then I saw an empty pill bottle on the floor which just seemed weird. I don't know why, but I walked around to the other side of the bed…"

He had to get it out; he took a deep breath, "She was there, just lying there on her side. It looked like she was sleeping but I knew she wasn't. I ran out of the room and left Jacob screaming. I went to the kitchen and dialed 911. I had learned about it from TV."

He took another long drink of his water, "I couldn't go back in the room. Jacob was screaming so loud, but I couldn't go back. I just sat in the kitchen and waited."

Trevor now noticed how much his leg was shaking. "Finally, the ambulance came and the paramedics rushed into mom's room. Then, this nice lady got Jacob out of his crib. She took my hand and led us out to her car. She told me we would be staying with another family for a while, just until Mom could get better."

"Was that your foster family?"

"Yeah. They were nice enough people, but they had three kids of their own. I just kind of felt like a stranger there, like I didn't belong. And I knew we would be going back to mom, so I didn't want to get too close to them anyway."

Dr. Fisher nodded, "And how were things after that, after you went back to stay with your mom?"

Trevor tilted the water bottle from side to side, watching the bubbles slosh around inside. *How were things?* Could he even put it into words? He would try.

He looked Dr. Fisher straight in the eye, "In one word—Hell."

CHAPTER 34

Slam!

The front door banged shut, and Trevor jumped up in his bed. *God damn it…every time!* He glanced over at Jacob's bed. The little guy had flipped over onto his stomach, but the noise didn't wake him. Fortunately Jacob was a heavy sleeper. Trevor wasn't so lucky.

This had become a nightly occurrence. Sometime between three and four in the morning, one of Mom's 'friends' would leave their house, the storm door always slamming behind them. Trevor had tried everything to block it out—pillow over the head, earplugs, earmuffs— nothing worked.

Two days ago he had tried to fix the door so that it wouldn't slam. That was a big mistake. He took an old dishtowel and taped it to the edge of the door hoping it would eliminate the clang of metal on metal. When mom saw it she went ballistic. "Trevor! What in the hell is this?!"

Trevor kept his eyes on the dirty floor, "I thought maybe I could fix the door. It slams really loud sometimes when I'm trying to sleep."

Mom snickered, "Oh it does?" She grabbed his face by the chin and forced him to look at her. She was wearing the wicked grin Trevor had seen so much of lately. "Well, genius, if you didn't notice, now the door doesn't shut completely. I can't have that door open all the time. Take it off now!"

Trevor got down on his knees and started ripping into the duct tape he had wrapped around the towel. Out of nowhere, something sharp hit him in the head. Pain radiated through the side of his face, and he saw a pair of scissors fall to the floor in front of him. He reached up to feel the spot that hurt so bad—just a little blood.

"It's barely a scratch! You're going to need those scissors. Just cut the damn towel up! It's ruined now anyway!" She was still shouting loud enough to make Trevor cringe. He knew a slap across the face could be coming next.

"Now I'm going out. If that door isn't the way you found it when I get back, there will be hell to pay." She grabbed her purse and walked past him, her high heels clicking against the tile, missing his hand by inches.

As she walked out the door, she yelled with her back still turned, "And if you could sleep like a normal kid, you wouldn't have to worry about the slamming!"

That was the day Trevor realized he would have to suffer through a lot of sleepless nights. Mom wasn't lying; he definitely didn't sleep like he should. But he thought he had some pretty good reasons why he couldn't sleep.

For one, he had to take care of Jacob which was a pain in the ass. After Mom would leave at night, he had to get Jacob a sippy-cup. He had to read Jacob a story, and then he usually had to rub Jacob's back until he fell asleep. Oh, and Jacob slept in Trevor's room, so if he ever woke up in the middle of the night, Trevor had to deal with it—not Mom.

Of course she was too busy. Mom went out every night, and when she came home, she always brought a man back with her. The walls were thin in their house and he would have to listen to the awful sounds coming from Mom's room. He would put his pillow over his head and sing to himself, but it never blocked it out completely. He was only ten, but he knew exactly what they were doing, and it made his stomach hurt.

Tonight Trevor pushed the bad thoughts out of his head and thought about Dad. Maybe he would come back—it had only been a couple of years. Trevor imagined him bursting through the front door one day, "Hey buddy let's go to a baseball game! I got tickets behind home plate for the Indian's game!" He replayed these thoughts over and over in his head as he tossed and turned in bed. Suddenly he was startled by shouting.

It was mom. "You son of a bitch! I told you it was twenty! This is a ten!"

Then he heard a man yell, "What are you going to do about it bitch?"

Crashing noises came from Mom's bedroom. Trevor's heart sank as he heard Mom scream, "No! No! I'm sorry, don't hurt me!"

Oh no! What should he do? Should he try to help mom? Should he hide? Trevor looked over at Jacob who was starting to move around but was still asleep. He had to protect his little brother.

He slowly opened his bedroom door a crack to peek out into the hallway. A gigantic bald man covered in tattoos was leaning over Mom with his fist in the air.

Trevor crept into the hallway and froze, terrified and unable to find his voice. Mom looked really bad. She had no shirt on and her face was red and puffy. She was trying really hard to get away, but the man was too powerful. Trevor tried to muster up his bravest voice, "Hey! Leave my mom alone!"

His shaky words came out in almost a whisper, but it was loud enough for the man to hear. He looked over at Trevor and then dropped mom to the ground like a bag of groceries, "What the hell? You have a kid here? You sick bitch!"

Mom was crying really hard now, and the bald man seemed even angrier. He stopped for a minute and stared at Trevor, his huge body heaving up and down with each breath.

To Trevor's immense relief, he just hurried down the hall and out the front door.

Slam!

***

Silence filled the air as Trevor paused a minute to catch his breath. Dr. Fisher was shaking her head, "Wow. I am so sorry you had to go through that Trevor."

Trevor felt a twinge of anger stir inside of him, "No. Please don't feel sorry for me, okay? That's the worst. I don't want pity from you, or anybody."

"It's not pity Trevor. There is a difference in feeling sorry about something that happened to a person, and feeling sorry *for* a person. That is pity. But I understand where you're coming from and it's noted. Did things change after that night?"

Trevor thought about it. That night probably was the turning point. "Yea, now that I think about it, that's when mom stopped going out. I guess she realized it wasn't worth getting beat up over."

He took the last sip of his water. "Her eye was all black and blue for weeks—that's when she really began hiding in her bedroom. She rarely came out for anything. I would feed Jacob and then put him in his playpen until I got home from school. He didn't get fed again or changed until I got home. He was never potty-trained and just stayed in diapers."

Trevor squeezed the empty water bottle, crushing it in his grip, "Jacob didn't like his playpen, and I was always worried he would get out. But every morning I would put him in there and hope for the best. I had to go to school or mom said the family services people would come snooping around."

Dr. Fisher looked especially bothered by this part of the story. She seemed to be at a loss for words, "How did you eat?" she finally asked.

"Actually, I remember this guy Tony used to come deliver groceries to us. Mom had some kind of arrangement with him." He shook his head, "Man, did we get the bare necessities."

Trevor counted them off on his fingers as he said them, "Bread, milk, a jar of peanut butter, potatoes, Cheerios, bottled water, rice, Saltines, toilet paper, a bar of soap, and of course, the two most important things, kleenex and cigarettes. Same thing every time."

"So I assume your mother was on government assistance?"

Trevor shrugged, "Yeah, I guess. She got a check in the mail and she wasn't quote, 'working' anymore, so yeah I guess we were on welfare."

Dr. Fisher nodded, "Hey I have an idea. Do you want to get a bite to eat? We can keep talking over some lunch." She looked at her watch, "Well, a late lunch anyway. You know, a change of scenery."

Trevor was getting hungry and his stomach had started rumbling. He finally had his appetite back but didn't want to stop the story. He didn't know if he would ever have the courage to finish it, if he didn't do it right then. "Yeah, I guess I could probably use some food."

***

Dr. Fisher swore this deli had the best corned-beef you'd ever tasted. Trevor must not have mentioned he was a vegetarian. He ordered the egg salad instead. The deli was noisy with the late lunch crowd, but they managed to get a quiet booth by the corner window. He took a large bite into the egg salad sandwich. It was delicious.

As he chewed, he looked out the window at the busy people passing by. Everyone looked so normal, so transparent. But like Dr. Fisher had told him, things aren't always as they seem. He bet most of them were carrying around some kind of baggage that stressed them out.

They ate their sandwiches in silence. Trevor took another sip of his Coke, "You know, if you have somewhere to go or something, please go. I don't want to take up your whole day or anything."

Dr. Fisher smiled, "When you called me from the hospital this morning, I cancelled all of my appointments for the day. You sounded like you really wanted to talk, and I'm glad you have. We can take as much time as you need. If you're still up to it."

"Yeah, I feel like if I don't talk about it now, I never will. You know?"

"So, you were taking care of your brother, Jacob?" She coaxed.

Thoughts of sippy-cups and shitty diapers raced through his mind. "I was taking care of him, and then Allison."

"Your baby sister?"

"Yeah. One day, my mom called me into her bedroom to tell me the wonderful news, about her miracle baby. She said it was—get this—a gift from God because there was no daddy. Obviously, I wasn't that naïve. Her friend Tony, the grocery guy, he took her to the hospital when she had the baby. Maybe he was the father. That was the only time I ever remember Mom leaving the house in like years."

Trevor took another bite of his sandwich, "Mom kept Allison in the bedroom with her like she did with Jacob. Then when Allison was about a year old, I took over—just like I did with Jacob. I fed her, changed her, and then stuck her in a playpen."

He went on, "In middle school, we were able to go home for lunch if we wanted so I started doing that every day. Jacob learned to sit quietly on the couch and watch his cartoons until I got home. Allison was a good baby, not as hyper as Jacob. She didn't mind the playpen at all. I would feed them lunch quickly and then hurry back to school." Then Trevor mocked in a stern voice, "Mom was not to be bothered."

Dr. Fisher sighed, "Such unbelievable neglect."

"Yeah, I guess we were used to it. We didn't know anything different." Trevor knew he was coming to the darkest point in his story—the memory that he couldn't bear to think about. He looked around the busy diner. "Do you think we could take a walk somewhere?"

"Sure, there's a little park at the corner. Why don't we go there?"

Dr. Fisher paid the tab and they headed for the park. As they walked side by side, she mentioned some of the quaint shops around the Beaumont Center. Trevor wasn't listening; all he could think about was the next part of his story.

This was the part he feared the most. This was the part that was so hidden in the depths of his mind, he never thought about it, let alone talked about it. This was why the man-in-black haunted his dreams, and he was about to re-live it all.

CHAPTER 35

"Trevor! Trevor I need you!" He heard the yelling coming from Mom's bedroom. *Shit.* He had five minutes to get on his bike and get his ass to school. One more tardy and it meant detention.

"Just a second!" He yelled back from the kitchen.

Jacob and Allison looked up from their empty cereal bowls. "She probably wants cigarettes." Jacob said matter-of-factly. He knew way too much for a six year old. Trevor poured Cheerios into their bowls and handed them spoons.

"What about the milk?" Jacob asked.

"Trevor!" Mom bellowed again from down the hall.

"Look, I can't get milk until tomorrow when mom gets her check. Just deal with it!" He reached over the top of the refrigerator and grabbed a pack of Viceroys out of the carton.

Allison started crying. "I want milk!" she sobbed.

Trevor was about to lose it. He was thirteen years old, not thirty!

"What about oatmeal then?" Jacob yelled.

"Just hold on!" he screamed over his shoulder. "I have to boil water—I don't have time for that!" *Jesus, they were bad off.* The people in his neighborhood were pretty poor, but he would bet they all had a microwave!

Trevor walked into the dark hallway that led to Mom's room. Her bedroom door was only opened a crack, but the cigarette smoke was seeping out. He could feel his chest tightening up—not so much from the noxious air, but more from his anxiety at seeing Mom. Every day she looked worse.

He slowly pushed the door open and peered inside. The room was dark. A heavy wool blanket covered the only window. Mom liked to keep it dark because it was easier to see the TV. She watched TV all day long—game shows and nothing else.

"Well don't just stand there stupid! Come here," she waved him over to her bedside.

As he took a step, his knees began shaking and his eyelid began twitching. *Get a hold of yourself Trevor.* He took a deep breath of the foul air and walked forward. He made sure to stop at arms-length away from mom. She didn't want anyone coming near her, not even her children.

He handed her the pack of Viceroys wrapped in a tissue. She carefully pulled the box away and threw the kleenex onto one of the growing piles next to her bed.

215

She immediately struck a match and took a long drag of the cigarette.

Mom was around thirty-five years old. She looked like she was in her sixties. Her face was sunken in and full of wrinkles. Her filthy, thin hair was slicked back and wrapped in a handkerchief. Deep lines surrounded her lips, partially because of the smoking, but also because Mom didn't eat—literally.

Trevor would offer her food all the time but she wanted only two things: bottled water and occasionally some crackers. She had begun losing her teeth. Trevor had noticed the first one about a year ago, a big black hole when she smiled. Now she had lost most of the ones in front.

"Empty that for me." Sitting on the bedside table was a paper plate with a mound of cigarette butts. It was only one day's worth. Almost half of mom's check money went to cigarettes. It was part of the reason Allison couldn't have milk in her cereal.

"Yes Mom," he picked up the teetering plate and turned to the door.

"Trevor," Mom called from behind.

He didn't turn around, "Yes?"

"I love you stupid," she said quietly.

***

Trevor looked up at Dr. Fisher. "I just remembered that."

"Which part?" she asked.

"That she told me she loved me. That was the first time."

Dr. Fisher nodded. "And what happened after that?"

Trevor closed his eyes. "I just went to school I guess."

"Well why don't you walk me through it?"

Trevor got up from the park bench and turned to Dr. Fisher. "I know I told you I wanted to talk about this, but now…I don't know if I can." No one had really heard about this part of his life. He just didn't know if he could get the words out.

He looked across the park at a little boy running through the trees with his mom. He was laughing and clapping happily. Is that what childhood was supposed to be like?

Dr. Fisher's voice was calm and reassuring, "Trevor I know this is very hard for you and you've been really brave so far. If you need to stop, I understand. I will always be here for you to talk to."

Something stirred inside him. Maybe telling her would alleviate some of the pain—some of the burden. He was sick of being the only human being on the planet who knew the whole story. He might as well just do it now.

The blue sky was tinged with the pink of dusk. Across the park the mom was hugging her little boy. He took another deep breath, "I went back to the kitchen."

***

"Are you leaving?" Allison asked, propped up on the couch in front of the TV.

Trevor grabbed his backpack off the floor. "I've got to go to school sweetie but I'll be back before you know it. I'll come home at lunch and make you some pb&j. How does that sound?"

She looked up at him with her big blue eyes and goofy grin. It killed him to have to leave her. She was only three years old, but was especially small for her age. He bent down and gave her a hug. "Be good and I will be back in just a couple of hours."

He walked into the kitchen where Jacob sat eating his dry cereal. "This is gross. I want oatmeal!"

Trevor ignored him, "Jacob, keep an eye on your sister. I'll be back at lunchtime and you make sure you're ready for the bus."

Jacob went to afternoon kindergarten, and that's when Trevor would try to get Allison down for a nap. At least when she was in the playpen she couldn't get into anything. Being home with mom was like being home alone.

Trevor pedaled hard the whole way to school, which happened to be over a mile away. A bus came by his house every morning, but because he had to come home on his lunch hours, the bike was his only option

The morning dragged on as it usually did. Sitting in his last class of the morning he thought about Allison and the look on her face when he left. The guilt started to set in and then quickly turned to anger when he thought about mom.

Trevor looked around at the other kids in the class and wondered what their moms were like. They probably had moms that helped with their homework and made their lunches. He would bet no one else had a mother like his.

The lunch bell rang out and he quickly threw his math folder and pencil into his backpack. He took off for his bike and started the trek home.

He was halfway to his house and turning down Beachwood when he heard them. Sirens—lots of them. The faster he pedaled, the louder they got.

Then in the distance, he saw black smoke rising up over the trees. *Jesus, it looked like it was coming from his neighborhood. It looked like it was coming from his street.*

Trevor pedaled faster as the panic set in. A large knot immediately formed in the pit of his stomach. When he got to his street, the knot felt like a fist that someone had thrust into him at full force. He almost couldn't believe what he was seeing.

Amidst the mass of blue and red flashing lights, a large crowd had gathered in front of *his* house. Trevor looked to both sides of the crowd—the run-down yellow duplex stood on the left, and Mrs. Perkin's cat-infested bungalow stood on the right. This was definitely where he lived, but there was no house. All he could see was a pile of black rubble smoldering in its place.

Things began moving in slow motion. His feet were moving forward like they were on auto-pilot. He looked around at the crowd of people. Their mouths were moving, but he couldn't hear anything. It was almost as if he was floating under water.

He found himself moving toward the lights where a man dressed in a black suit stood talking to a group of police officers. They didn't notice him in all of the chaos, and as Trevor got closer, the sound of the man's voice became clear.

Trevor stood next to the man-in-black, and looked up at his face as he spoke. The words trickled down to him like tiny knives stabbing him in his heart, "It looks like a gas explosion from inside—probably the stove. We have three bodies, one adult and two children. They never had a chance."

With those words, Trevor fell to his knees and screamed, until he couldn't scream anymore.

CHAPTER 36

Trevor took a deep breath, "And that's what happened." He slowly looked up at Dr. Fisher, not sure what to expect.

He could see the pity on her face, "Trevor, that was really gutsy. I'm proud of you."

His feelings of guilt started creeping in and then the anger, "Proud? Seriously? I left those kids to fend for themselves and they died!"

The whole thing was too much. He felt like he was going to explode. He stood up from the bench and began pacing.

Then he started yelling, "It's my fault Dr. Fisher! Don't you get it! I left those kids alone! I should've been there!" He fell back onto the bench and lowered his head.

And then Trevor began sobbing—four years of feelings flowing out of him—an outpouring of bottled up anger, grief, and guilt. "I wish I was home that day. I just wish I would've died."

Dr. Fisher put her arm around him, "Here," she handed him a tissue. "Trevor, I know you've heard this before but this was *not* your fault. You have to know that. The investigators determined it was a deliberate act by your mother."

He had to say what had bothered him for years, what he was too afraid to tell anyone. "I've gone over this a million times in my head, okay? When I left, Jacob wanted oatmeal. He tried to make it himself and turned that stove on—he left it on. It was my fault!"

Dr. Fisher put her hands on Trevor's shoulders and turned to face him. "Look at me Trevor. I know it's hard to hear this, but this was only one person's fault—your mother's."

He needed reassurance, "But you don't understand. She never got out of bed! Ever! She never would've turned the stove on."

She sighed, "Trevor, even if that was the case, it is still your mother's fault. It was not your job to raise those children. It was her job. Look at me."

Trevor's eyes were blurry from the tears but he tried to look her in the face. He could trust her—he felt it. For some reason he knew Dr. Fisher wouldn't lie to him.

"Your mom told you that she loved you. You said she had never done that before—why that day? It may very well be the case that she was saying goodbye."

This thought swirled around in his head. Could Mom really have done this? Trevor had always blamed himself—always.

"No. I mean why didn't she just take a bunch of pills, like she did last time? Why this way? Why would she have to take them with her? It doesn't make any sense. How could she do that to them? How could she do that to me?" He searched Dr. Fisher's face for answers.

"I don't have an answer for that. Trevor, your mom was obviously a very ill woman. No one will ever know what was going through her mind." She continued, "Even you will never really know."

He was hearing what Dr. Fisher was saying, but he just couldn't find himself to accept it. Mom was crazy about a lot of things, but to do something like this? He couldn't wrap his head around it.

"The one thing you have to know is that this is not your fault. You are the victim in this—the victim. You've endured a childhood that no one should." She reached over and grabbed his hand, "And in spite of it all, you're living a very admirable life."

The emotions were overwhelming. He truly didn't know what to think anymore.

Then Dr. Fisher asked him something that seemed to come out of left field, "Trevor, have you ever thought about why you garbage pick? I mean, what really motivates you?"

Trevor thought about it, "Well, my uncle made me start garbage-picking so I could 'earn my keep' and then…"

"And then?"

"And then I guess I liked finding things I could fix—that didn't have to be thrown away. It's better for the environment, you know, less in a landfill. And I love giving toys to the kids at Haven House."

The sun was setting over the horizon and people were starting to leave the park. "And certainly, that is all true. But I have a theory about your subliminal motivation for garbage-picking. You want to hear it?"

"Wow, my subliminal motivation?" He actually did want to hear it. "Sure, okay doc…tell me." He was curious now.

"I think when you drive down the street and you see something on the curb, you see more than just garbage. For example, you see that wheelbarrow, missing a wheel. You know that all it needs is a new wheel, and it will be like new." She paused, "You know that wheelbarrow isn't trash, and it doesn't belong in a dump. You know that someone, somewhere, will really appreciate that wheelbarrow. It just needs a little fixing and a new home."

She put her arm around his shoulder and gave him a quick squeeze. "That wheelbarrow just needs a chance. You are giving that wheelbarrow hope."

Trevor could feel the emotions swelling up inside of him, "Hope for garbage, huh?"

"Yeah, I guess you could say that. Hope for garbage."

Dr. Fisher seemed to be able to read him like no one else could. But weirdly enough, it didn't scare him. It only made him feel more comfortable around her.

Now he was totally exhausted, but in a good way. "Well, thanks a lot for listening to all my stuff. I guess I kind of wasted your whole day."

Dr. Fisher smiled, "Absolutely not. I am so glad we had this talk. You've been really brave."

As the darkness settled in, the park got quiet and crickets began chirping. Talking to Dr. Fisher about the past was something he didn't think he'd ever be able to do. But now that he had, he felt so much better.

"Well, we should probably be heading back now," she said.

"Yeah," Trevor agreed, "And do you think I could ask you for one more favor?"

"Sure Trevor, anything."

"Do you think you could wheel me over to Lorene's house?"

CHAPTER 37

Lorene looked around her son Brian's room. The Cleveland Browns posters still covered the walls and his drum set still sat in the corner. She had kept it pretty much how he'd left it when he went off to college—with one big exception—now it was clean. Hopefully, Trevor would feel at home here. God knows what kinds of conditions that poor kid had lived in. He deserved better.

Lorene was excited, but nervous as well. She had asked Reggie to run to the grocery store and pick up some snacks and things a teenager would like. Of course she reminded him that Trevor was a vegetarian, so no pepperoni pizza or any of those Slim Jims that Reggie loved so much.

Just then Lorene heard a car pull up out front. She peeked out the bedroom window but it was only Reggie returning with the groceries. She hurried downstairs to greet him. "You need any help hon?"

Reggie put his hands up. "No, no. You know the drill. I'll bring all of the bags in. You just put everything away."

Lorene took the gallon of milk that Reggie was holding and put it in the fridge. As Reggie put the bags on the kitchen table, Lorene unloaded them. Reggie might've gone a little overboard. She didn't know where she was going to put all of this stuff!

She was moving things around in the refrigerator when she felt someone standing behind her. "You need something out of here Reggie?" she asked over her shoulder.

No answer. She turned around to find it wasn't Reggie at all. Trevor was standing there with a bag of groceries and a smile on his face. "Hey Lorene."

She stood up, and without even thinking about it, stretched her arms out in front of her. "Trevor! Welcome to our home!" He gave her a quick hug and she was shocked by how thin and frail he felt. This boy needed to eat! "Hon, you sit right there at that table. I am going to make you a late snack!"

He didn't look very interested. "I just ate a little bit ago. I'm not really hungry, just tired."

It was his first night there, so Lorene decided not to push it. "Okay. Why don't I show you around real quick? Then you can get some sleep."

He yawned, "That sounds great. Thanks."

***

"Trevor! Wake up!" He could feel someone shaking his shoulder as he slowly opened his eyes. Everything was out of focus at first. Finally he was able to make out Lorene, standing above him with a big smile on her face.

"What time is it?" he asked groggily.

She walked over to the window and cranked the blinds open. "I'm sorry hon. I never would've woken you but I thought for sure you'd be up by now. It's almost 1:30 and I told Carol Sorak she could come over. She's been taking care of your dog for you."

Jip! Trevor sat up in bed and shielded his eyes from the light. He couldn't wait to hug the little guy. "Are you sure it will be okay to have Jip here?"

She smiled, "Of course. Reggie and I have had a few dogs in our time, so we know what to expect. Besides, I know how much he means to you. It will be fine."

She paused by the door, "Oh and there are towels in the tall cabinet next to the sink. And I made you some homemade mac and cheese—the good stuff, not that Kraft junk. It's in the fridge."

"Okay, thanks." Lorene was being unbelievably nice. He wasn't used to this.

Once she was out of the room, Trevor pulled himself out of bed and headed for the shower. He stood under the hot water, trying to wash away some of the sleepiness. It wasn't working.

Maybe eating something some would help. He went down to the kitchen and got the mac and cheese out of the fridge. He popped it in the microwave and poured himself a glass of milk. He was sitting down at the table when he heard a dog bark out front. *Jip!*

He dropped his fork and ran out the front door. Before he could step off the porch Jip was in his lap, yelping and licking his face frantically. "Okay boy, okay…" Tears were forming in Trevor's eyes. He couldn't help it. This was their dog, his and Mr.T's. The licking and whimpering continued as Trevor buried his face in Jip's fur. "I missed you too."

"Hello Trevor." He hadn't even noticed Carol Sorak standing there. She was smiling, but there was sadness in her eyes.

Trevor stood up, putting Jip on the ground. "Hey Carol."

She put her arms out and hugged him, squeezing him hard. They were both missing Mr.T. "How are you holding up?" she asked.

Trevor noticed her eyes watering, and he only hoped she didn't lose it right there. He knew that if she started crying, he would start crying too. "Okay, I guess. It's really nice being here, with Lorene."

Carol nodded, "She seems like a really nice lady."

"Hey thank you so much for taking care of Jip. I was so relieved when they told me he was with you. I can't thank you enough."

"Oh that was nothing. He was no trouble at all." She smiled down at Jip who had not left Trevor's side. "Hey guess what else I brought ya?"

Trevor only hoped she was talking about one thing.

She walked back to the car, opened the door and pulled out a silver pot so big, she could barely get her arms around it. Trevor rushed to her aid and grabbed the pot out of her hands.

He could already feel his stomach grumbling as the familiar aroma rose from the pot. "Cabbage and noodles?" he asked with a smile.

"Yep, the one and only."

"Two things that can make me happy no matter what—Jip and Cabbage & Noodles. Thanks so much Carol. For everything."

She put her hands on Trevor's shoulders, "Just promise me you will come by the diner once in a while. I know it's a little out of your way now, but I'd still like to see my favorite patron. You hear?"

"I promise."

She gave him another hug and then Carol walked back to her car.

He turned to make his way back to the house when Jip started barking like crazy. Trevor looked over his shoulder to see what the dog was yapping about.

Just as Carol pulled away, a black sedan pulled up in the driveway. Trevor stood like a statue, holding the giant pot in front of him.

As the car door opened, he felt his grip slipping on the pot. Out came Investigator O'Donnell, a.k.a. the man-in-black.

CHAPTER 38

Trevor set the pot down on the grass and wiped his hands on his jeans. What the hell did he want?

The man-in-black wasn't wearing black this time. He approached Trevor wearing khakis, a blue button-down, and a big smile on his face. "Hi Trevor, I have some good news for you."

As Investigator O'Donnell stood in front of him, Trevor realized he wasn't very tall. In fact, he was shorter than Trevor. As a kid, the man-in-black had seemed like a giant. And from the hospital bed, he had seemed much more intimidating. Not so much today; he looked more like Trevor's history teacher.

"Good news. Really?" Trevor was surprised at how calm his own voice sounded.

"Yeah, I just heard on the wire that they caught your uncle. Someone spotted his truck at a roach motel in southern Indiana. They apprehended him about an hour ago."

Mixed emotions swirled around inside Trevor. He was happy they caught the bastard, but he really didn't want to deal with all the legal bullshit that would be coming down soon. "That's good," Trevor said.

"I bet you're relieved."

Did he think Trevor was afraid of the fat-ass? "Relieved? Not really, just glad the asshole will get what's coming to him."

Investigator O'Donnell nodded, "Well I'm sure the police will be contacting you shortly." He reached inside his jacket and pulled out a folded up piece of paper. "I also wanted to give you something."

He held the paper in front of Trevor, "Before you read this, you need to know that there is someone out there who really cares about you. I could get into deep shit here, but you have a very persuasive friend." He handed the paper to Trevor, "Anyway, I think this may clarify some things for you. And if you have any questions, my numbers on there." He handed a business card to Trevor, and turned to leave.

"Uh, thanks." Trevor felt a twinge of anxiety creep into his gut.

As Investigator O'Donnell got in his car and pulled away, Trevor slowly opened the folded up piece of paper. Large black lettering across the top of the paper read:

OFFICIAL FINDINGS: Case 54792-b   09/2010
MCNULTY, PAULA

The twinge of anxiety spread like a wave that sent his heart racing and his palms sweating once again. He crumpled up the paper and shoved it in his pocket.

He ran into the house, not looking back. With his stomach in knots, he forgot all about the pot of cabbage and noodles sitting on the front lawn.

***

Trevor sat on the edge of his bed and pulled out the crumpled piece of paper from his pocket. He took a deep breath. He desperately wanted to know what happened in his house that day, but he was so afraid.

He closed his eyes and tried to remember what Dr. Fisher had said to him, "This was not your fault."

Screw it. He slowly opened the paper and began reading:

It is the official finding of this investigation that the fire was started by a gas explosion from the gas stove in the kitchen. It is determined the gas leaked for an extended period of time where occupants were aware of leak because breathing would have become difficult. It is determined that ignition occurred in close proximity to gas stove (within 1-2 feet). The fire was ignited by a small flame source, and given supporting case evidence, the source was likely a lighter, match, or lit cigarette. Based on burn patterns and body location, all three victims appeared to be in close range of explosion at time of ignition, with adult female closest to the source of ignition. All windows and doors in the home appeared to be locked from the inside. It is highly unlikely the ignition was accidental, as occupants would have left residence because of lack of oxygen.

The official conclusion of this investigation is as follows: Fire was started by intentional gas leak and intentional ignition of leak, by one Paula McNulty.

The official ruling of this investigation: Double homicide; suicide.

Trevor stared down at the paper, his eyes focused on one phrase that was highlighted in bright yellow marker*: with adult female closest to source of ignition.*

Mom did it. She was right by the stove—she was out of bed. She let the gas run until they couldn't breathe, and she locked them in.

Trevor suddenly felt something lurch inside his stomach, a sickening realization of what mom had done. It was too much to take. *No, no, no…*

"No!" he screamed.

He ran to the bathroom and threw his body over the toilet. His body heaved up and down until every bit of gut-wrenching vomit was finally expelled. Trevor laid his head on the seat of the toilet and closed his eyes.

"No, mom, no." Then he collapsed into a heap of sobs.

CHAPTER 39

It was Trevor's second day at Lorene's house. So far, it had been quiet compared to the first. Not that he was complaining. He wouldn't mind having one day with no visitors at all. He was already exhausted and it was only late afternoon. The stress must really be catching up with him, because he hadn't done much of anything today.

Earlier he had watched TV for a while, and then he helped Reggie on his train cars. While painting the old cars Trevor was reminded of the Box. All of his tools, his projects, his ideas—up in smoke, literally.

He was now in his new room putting away the few clothes he had. He liked this room; it didn't smell. And he couldn't get over how clean everything was. He didn't have to worry about things crawling on him in his sleep, or the disgusting toilet that overflowed on a regular basis.

He would never have to step inside Uncle Gary's rat hole again.

Trevor couldn't wait for the day when he got to face his uncle again. Imagining him all decked out in an orange jumpsuit and cuffs made Trevor smile.

There was sure to be a trial. Uncle Gary would never confess or make a deal. But that didn't bother Trevor. He planned on being there for every minute of it.

That day played over and over in his head. It was still hard to believe that the whole thing had happened at all. He knew his Uncle Gary had a screw loose—there was no doubt about that. But to come at Trevor with an axe and leave him to burn? That was a whole new level of crazy. Trevor could only hope the bastard would get what he deserved.

"Knock, knock…" It was Lorene.

"Come in!"

Lorene was always smiling, "Hey, I forgot to tell you that Jean Tyminski will be stopping by in a little bit— Mr.Tyminski's daughter."

Really?

Trevor's heart sank at the thought of Mr.T. It still didn't seem real. He felt uneasy about meeting Mr.T's family. What if she blamed him?

Lorene set a glass of ice water on the bedside table. "If you're thirsty…It's a hot one today."

She must have seen the worry on Trevor's face, "Jean came to see me a couple of days ago, and said she really wanted to meet you. I wouldn't have invited her over without giving you more notice, but she has a flight back to California tomorrow. I meant to tell you last night, but you looked so exhausted. And you went up to bed so early."

Trevor wished he could just hide in this room forever, just pull the covers up over his head and never come out. "Did she say what she wanted to talk about?"

Lorene sighed, "Not specifically. But she said very nice things about you Trevor. She said her father talked about you all the time, and thought of you as a grandson. She seemed like a very nice person."

Trevor tried to feel some comfort in Lorene's words, but his anxiety was growing.

Suddenly Jip jumped on the bed and began barking. Someone was here.

Lorene got up, "Oh, I'm going to go get the door. That's probably her now."

Shit. He felt very strange about meeting Mr.T's daughter. Her dad was gone because of him. Trevor just hoped she wasn't going to ask him questions about what happened that day, because he honestly didn't have the answers.

As he walked down the stairs, his shoulders relaxed. Jean Tyminski was standing across from Lorene in the entryway, in shorts and a t-shirt. She had a big smile on her face and seemed friendly enough. The conversation suddenly stopped as they turned their attention to him.

Lorene quickly made introductions, "Trevor, this is Jean Tyminski, Mr.Tyminski's daughter."

Jean reached her hand to Trevor, "It's so nice to finally meet you Trevor. My dad talked about you all the time."

He nodded, "Hi."

"Well I better go check on dinner. Jean, can I get you something to drink?" Lorene asked.

Jean held up an aluminum water bottle, "No, I'm fine really." *Finally someone carrying a responsible water bottle!*

"I think we'll go outside if that's okay with you Trevor?"

"Yeah, that's fine."

It was hot as hell outside—probably in the nineties, and humid too. But inside the house, it was just as bad. Lorene didn't have air conditioning and preferred it that way. She said she liked the heat. It was the only time her arthritis didn't bother her. She offered to buy Trevor a window unit for his room if he wanted it. But like Lorene, he didn't mind the heat. After having the kind of winter they did, he would never complain.

"Why don't we go sit on the porch?" Jean asked.

Two white wicker chairs took up most of the space on the small covered porch. Colorful flower baskets hung from the wood ceiling. Like the rest of Lorene's house, it was very cozy.

They sat down and Trevor tried to make himself comfortable. But the familiar, uncontrollable sensations came on fast. His heart began racing and his eyelid twitched. And the heat seemed to make his anxiety worse.

Before Jean could say anything, he heard himself rambling, "I just want you to know, I feel so bad about what happened to Mr.T. I can't believe that he risked his life for me. And he died for me! I am so sorry that this happened. I am so sorry—you don't know how sorry I am."

Trevor suddenly felt Jean's hand rest on his. As he glanced over at her, she was dabbing the corner of her eye with a tissue. "Trevor…please stop."

She smiled, "Please do not blame yourself for this. You meant the world to my dad. He talked about you all the time. He loved you like a grandson Trevor, he really did."

Trevor could feel the tears welling up inside of him. Thinking about Mr.T was too painful. He missed the old man so badly, it actually hurt inside physically.

He tried to focus on something—anything. He looked across the street at two little kids running through a sprinkler.

"After my mom died, my dad was in bad shape…really bad shape. My sister and I asked him to come out to California but he didn't want to move. He always said Cleveland was his home and that was that."

Jean went on, "Well, we even considered moving back here, but Dad wouldn't have it. He knew how much we loved it out there and he didn't want his grandchildren being moved around. He insisted we stay put—and so we did."

She reached into her bag and pulled out another aluminum water bottle. "God, it's hot." She handed it to Trevor, "Here—I brought one for you—ice water."

"Thanks," Trevor took a long drink, "I guess I must be used to the heat. It really doesn't bother me."

"Yeah, my dad told me that about you. He said you weren't a complainer." She took another drink, "Anyway, we would come visit twice a year and we would fly him out to see us twice a year. But he never seemed right, and understandably so. And truthfully, he was getting worse every year. We were all devastated by mom's passing, but my mom and dad had something really special."

She was quiet for a minute and Trevor was afraid she would start crying again. "We worried, a lot. Until you came along."

"Me?" Trevor asked.

She turned to face him. "Yes you Trevor. I can't tell you how much my dad changed after he met you. It was like he was a completely different person. When we had our weekly chat, I could hear the excitement in his voice."

Jean had a huge smile on her face now, "He loved telling me what you guys had done that week, what you were working on in the Box—all of it. It was such a relief to finally hear some happiness in his voice."

Trevor hadn't realized how much he had meant to Mr.T. He knew the old man cared about him, but neither of them were big on showing emotions. "Well, he always used to say to me, 'it goes both ways'. He definitely changed my life too."

Jean sat back in her chair, "Trevor, I have to tell you a little story so that all of this will make sense to you. Is that okay?"

Trevor wasn't sure exactly what 'all of this' was. Just when he was beginning to feel relaxed, the anxiety started creeping back in, "Okay…"

"Trevor, did my dad ever tell you…how my mom died?"

CHAPTER 40

Trevor was caught a little off guard, and he wasn't sure he wanted to hear about Mr.T's wife. "No, he didn't really talk about her."

The kids across the street were now filling up a baby pool shaped like a turtle. They were fighting over who got to hold the hose.

"Well I don't like talking about it, but I think I need to explain to you what happened. All of this will make more sense."

All of what? The tone of her voice changed and he thought he heard a twinge of anger in it. He had a feeling this wasn't going to be good. He took another long drink of his water.

"My mother had insomnia and it was pretty serious. People think it's just that insomniacs can't sleep well, but it's actually a medical condition and it can cause serious problems. If it's severe, as in my mother's case, it can cause heart problems—even diabetes. When my mom developed high blood pressure, she decided to get some help. She had always been very health conscience."

Jean paused and looked at Trevor, "I'm sorry to go on like this, it's just I feel like my dad would've wanted you to know everything."

"No, it's okay, really." Not really, but what choice did he have?

"Well, anyway, this was about the time they came out with all those new prescription sleep-aids. So my mom decided to try one called Zenban. She was on it for a few months and said it worked wonders.

"And then one morning my dad got up, and my mom was still sleeping. This was unusual, but he let her sleep in for a while. After a couple hours, he tried to wake her and she wouldn't get up."

Jean wiped her eyes, "He called 911 right away and she was rushed to the hospital. But it was too late—she had suffered a massive stroke and never recovered. She was in a coma for eight days before she passed away. My dad never left her side."

Trevor honestly didn't want to hear another word, but he had to ask. "What happened? Did it have something to do with the sleeping pills?"

"Yes. They did an autopsy and found out she had twenty times the effective ingredient in her system. Apparently there was some kind of manufacturing defect at the pharmaceutical plant and a very small batch of

Zenban was affected. They never told us exactly how it happened."

She sighed, "Three people died and five people were seriously ill from it. I think one of them is still in a coma to this day. The drug was immediately recalled and never went into production again—at least under that name. It made headlines for a day or two."

Trevor shook his head, "God, I feel so bad that Mr.T had to go through that. It's just unbelievable that something like that could happen."

"We were devastated—and so angry. It was just so senseless! All of the families filed suits against the pharmaceutical company. My father really wanted nothing to do with it. I think it was just too painful for him. But my sister and I were hell-bent on making someone pay, and the company wanted to avoid the bad press."

"Is the company still around?" he asked.

"Oh yes. It's one of the biggest, and doing very well I might add. My sister and I never regretted our decision. But it didn't make us feel any better about Mom…" Jean trailed off.

"Anyway, my dad never felt comfortable with the money. He gave half of it to my sister Kate and I. My sister is a financial planner so she basically managed it for both of us.

"And, they were building a new mental health center for children near Southwest General. Dad thought it was a worthy cause and he gave the rest to them."

Realization hit Trevor all at once. The one condition for Mr.T was that he went to the Beaumont Center for his sessions.

"The Beaumont Children's Center?" Trevor asked, already knowing the answer.

Jean smiled with a curious look, "Yes, Beaumont was my mother's maiden name. Do you know of it? It's a beautiful facility."

"Yeah, I've heard of it." Sneaky old man—no wonder he always knew whether or not Trevor went to his sessions. Mr.T paid for the damn place!

She went on, "My dad asked Kate to invest a small piece of the settlement as an emergency fund, or a just-in-case fund if you will. Well, my sister is an excellent investor, and the money grew into quite a sizable amount."

Trevor was trying to process everything he was hearing, "But Mr.T—your dad—never acted like he had money. I mean, he didn't have any fancy cars or anything. I never would've guessed it."

Jean reached out and grabbed both of his hands. "He never wanted the money Trevor." Her face lit up, "But he did want you to have it."

"Me?" He was confused.

"Trevor, my father left you eight hundred thousand dollars."

CHAPTER 41

"So what do you think they're talking about?" Lorene whispered over to Reggie as she peeked out the front window. Trevor and Jean still appeared to be in deep discussion on the front porch.

"Why are you whispering woman? They can't hear you." Reggie shook his head and went back to eating his chicken salad sandwich.

"It's been almost an hour. What could they be talking about? I thought I heard her say something about Tom's wife. What could that be about?"

Reggie sighed, "I'm sure it's fine Lorene."

"Well, I know she can't be blaming Trevor for what happened to that poor man. Oh—!" She rushed back into her seat at the kitchen table. "Here he comes!" Lorene put her head down and pretended to read the junk mail that was splayed out in front of her.

Trevor walked in and quickly headed toward the staircase, avoiding Lorene's eyes. His face was flushed and he looked visibly upset. She noticed a large manila envelope in his hands.

"Hey Trevor!" she called after him. "You want me to make you a sandwich?"

He disappeared up the stairwell without answering. Lorene turned to Reggie, "I think he was crying. Did you see that?" she asked in a harsh whisper.

Reggie set down his sandwich, "Did I see what exactly?"

"I know. It's none of my business, right? That's what you're going to tell me?"

"No, I wasn't going to say that. Just give the kid some space. He's been through a lot, and I don't think there's anything wrong with letting him have a good cry once in a while."

Lorene knew Reggie was right. "Well, maybe I should just go up there and see if he needs anything."

"Lor--ene..." Reggie said with exaggerated emphasis.

"Oh, all right!" she said.

Just then there was a tap at the front door. Lorene had forgotten all about Jean. She quickly went to the door and opened it.

Jean looked just as upset as Trevor. "Hi Lorene, I just wanted to thank you again for everything. I know Trevor is in really good hands. My dad would be happy he was here with you."

"Well, we are so happy to have him." Lorene couldn't resist, "Did you guys have a good talk?"

Jean smiled, "Yes, a very good talk." She reached into her purse and handed Lorene a business card, "I'd like it if we could keep in touch—you know, just to see how he's doing."

"Of course! I would like that very much."

And with that, Jean Tyminski waved goodbye and was gone.

Reggie went back to finishing his sandwich and Lorene's mind immediately began to wander. It seemed like the conversation between Trevor and Jean had gone well, but...

She forced herself to go load the dishwasher and try not to worry about the boy. Lorene would give him some time. She just hoped Trevor could handle whatever he was going through right now.

***

Shit. His hands wouldn't stop shaking.

All of the legal paperwork from Mr. T's will and trust was in the envelope. Jean told him there were instructions on what to do to access his funds. *His funds!* There was also a list of financial people Jean recommended, who could help him if he needed it. Hell yes, he needed it.

And then there was the letter. Jean told him there was a letter from Mr. T.—a letter he had written to Trevor just days before he died.

But, he physically couldn't read it. He couldn't even bring himself to open it. His hands wouldn't let him.

So he laid down on his neatly made bed, the unopened letter sitting beside him. Looking up at the ceiling, he saw tiny glow-in-the dark stars scattered everywhere. He had been so exhausted the last couple of nights, he hadn't noticed them.

Lorene was obviously a great mom. No surprise there; she was a great person. Maybe he could just have Lorene read the letter to him. Without thinking about it too much, he opened the bedroom door and yelled down, "Lorene!"

Within seconds she was at his door, "Yes Trevor, you need something hon?"

He took a deep breath, "Yeah, if you don't mind…" He reached out and handed the letter to her, his hand still trembling. "Do you think you could read this to me?"

"Of course. I'd be glad to do that." She sat next to him on the bed, "You okay Trevor? Can I go get you something? A drink, or maybe something to eat?"

He could only imagine what he must look like, "No thanks. I just want you to read this for me, okay?" Trevor was trying to hold back his tears. He just hoped he could keep it together.

"Sure." And with that Lorene began reading the letter.

Trevor closed his eyes and listened…

Dear Trevor,

We both knew this day would come too soon. After my 'episode' in the hospital, I knew my ticker wasn't quite right and I thought maybe I should write you this letter. Don't be crying over me now kid – I am with my dearest Maddie and we are doing just fine.

By now, one of my wonderful daughters has told you about my gift to you. I know you pride yourself in your independence, but please accept it graciously. You saved me from some of my darkest days, and you know what I always told you…it goes both ways.

I know you won't run out and buy a Ferrari or anything. Use it to do what you have always done – use it for good.
I will be looking down and smiling. Just imagine how beautiful this planet would be if there were more people like YOU in it.

Make me proud kid.
Love, Mr.T

CHAPTER 42

One Year Later...

Lorene closed her eyes and let the warm summer sun touch her face. She rocked back and forth on the porch swing, smiling at the scene in front of her.

In the center of her backyard, Trevor, Reggie and Frank were unloading another delivery into the new and improved Box, or Box2, as Trevor liked to call it.

Construction on Box2 had just wrapped up a few weeks ago and it was quite a sight. It was about three times the size of the old Box, and it was state-of-the-art. Fitted with solar panels, wind turbines, and even a rain collection system, it was environmentally friendly as well.

From the outside it looked simply like a smaller version of Lorene's house. It had white vinyl siding with black shutters, an entry door, and a couple of windows.

But inside was a different story. The large space was impressive with soaring vaulted ceilings and skylights. All of the walls were lined with different stations—long tables set up with the best tools money could buy. There were stations for electrical work, carpentry, metal work and even plumbing.

But the painting room had to be Lorene's favorite part of Box2. This small separate room off the back was dedicated solely to painting. A large worktable stood in the center and shelves of brightly colored paint cans lined the walls. It was built with the most advanced ventilation system available, so even in the winter time, the air was always fresh. This was Reggie's room.

Shortly after Trevor came to live with them, Reggie helped the boy restore some old toys with a new paint job. It only took one visit to the Haven House for Reggie to realize he wanted to paint more than train cars. That man couldn't wait for Trevor to return from a pick. The first words out of his mouth were always, "Did you get any toys?"

What made Lorene smile most of all was the fact that Trevor had decided to attend college. Reserve University was only a twenty minute drive from Lorene's house, and it was one of the best engineering schools in the Midwest. He had decided to pursue a degree in environmental engineering and was starting in the fall.

He asked Lorene if it was okay to continue living with her through his first year of college. Of course she said "Yes." He was welcome as long as he liked. As far as Lorene was concerned, the longer Trevor stayed, the better.

Trevor wanted to keep working in Box2, but he realized most of his time would be taken up with his studies. He also realized that getting up at the crack of dawn to go picking wouldn't be feasible.

So he called his friend Frank and offered him a well-paying side job. When college started, Frank would do most of the garbage-picking for Trevor.

Lorene liked to help out as well. She would bring out sandwiches, help with deliveries, and check out the garage sales on Thursday mornings. Because she no longer worked for the Stewarts, she had a lot more time on her hands.

In the spring, after a long and nasty court battle, the Stewart's divorce was finalized. And the house went on the market last month. Mrs. Stewart ended up buying a condominium, still a prestigious lake address of course. Lorene had stayed on to help out with the packing and cleaning, and then it was time to say her goodbyes.

Leaving Bea was heart-wrenching, but the girl was off to a new chapter in her life. She was headed to Stanford in the fall to study psychology, of all things. Lorene had very high hopes for Bea, just like she did for Trevor.

She knew that Bea and Trevor had kept in touch. Bea admitted that they had talked a few times, but nothing ever came of it. Lorene still thought that was a tad surprising.

Immediately after Trevor was injured, Bea seemed so upset. Lorene thought for sure she must be in love with the boy. Then four days later, when Bea actually did see him in the hospital, she just broke it off. Lorene didn't expect that.

"Hey! Lorene!" She was startled out of her thoughts by shouts across the yard.

Carrying a cardboard box overflowing with books, Trevor walked toward her with Jip following at his heels. "Hey Lorene! Guess where these came from?"

"Where?" she yelled back.

"The Stewart's house!" Just then he stumbled and the box toppled over, spilling paperbacks all over the grass.

"Oh Lord, let me help you," Lorene rushed over to Trevor and kneeled down in the grass.

The boy had grown so much in a year, not just physically, but emotionally as well. He and Reggie liked to lift weights down in the basement together. Between Lorene's home cooking and that new hobby, the boy had filled out nicely. Scrawny old Trevor was long gone!

He had also been faithfully going to his sessions with Dr. Fisher. Now he seemed to be smiling all the time. He was almost a different person.

"Yea, Frank said they're getting rid of a lot of good stuff over there," he said.

Lorene reached over and picked up a Nicholas Sparks book. Romance novels were always Mrs. Stewart's favorite. She would draw little hearts in the margins like a teenage girl. The woman was crazy in a lot of ways, but she was a romantic at heart. She even kept—

Oh Lord. Why hadn't Lorene thought of it before? It would explain so much…

Evelyn Stewart kept a diary—and Bea knew exactly where it was hidden.

***

Lorene suddenly had a funny expression on her face. "Lorene? Is there something wrong?" Trevor asked.

"No, no, I think this summer heat is just getting to me." They finished picking up the books.

"Hey, you want to take a break?" Lorene asked. "You've been working too hard and you look beat. You want to go have some lemonade on the porch with me?"

"Yeah, that sounds great." Trevor made his way to the porch and collapsed onto the swing.

Lorene came back with two large glasses of lemonade. She made the homemade stuff too—just the perfect mixture of lemons, sugar and ice.

He took a long drink and closed his eyes as the icy liquid made its way down his throat, "Lorene, you make the best lemonade."

"Awe. Thank you hon," she said.

Trevor looked out at Box2. It was awesome. Reggie, Lorene, and Frank had all helped turn his dream into a reality. He would be able to keep garbage-picking and working in the box, doing what he loved. And he would be able to go to college, which he knew was the smartest thing to do.

He had offered to pay rent to Lorene. Hell, he had offered to pay off their mortgage. She and Reggie would have no part of it. They insisted that Trevor use his own money for his own dreams. Reggie and Lorene were just great people, no doubt about it.

Lorene was petting Jip on her lap. The two of them had become good buddies, "Things have turned out pretty great, huh Trevor?"

He smiled, "Yes, most definitely."

They sat quietly on the swing for a minute or two. Trevor closed his eyes and said a silent thank you to Mr.T. He was finally getting a break, in a big way, and he knew Mr.T was up there watching it all.

"Trevor, can I ask you about something?"

"Shoot," he took another sip of his lemonade.

"Well…" Lorene began. Her voice sounded strange. "I was just wondering…you know what? Just forget it."

Geez, this shy act wasn't like her at all. She almost sounded embarrassed. He laughed, "C'mon! You've got to ask me now!"

She held back for a couple more seconds and then blurted it out, "What really happened that night in Mrs. Stewart's Mercedes?"

Whoa. He wasn't expecting that. "Uh…"

Lorene stood up, "No! I'm sorry! You know what? Forget it. It is none of my business and it is not my place. Just forget I ever said anything."

She put Jip on the ground. "My curiosity is just getting the best of me. Sometimes I don't know when the heck to shut up. I'm sorry. Really Trevor—forget it."

He laughed, "No it's okay, really. Sit down." He didn't want to lie to Lorene. He really didn't. If there was one thing he had learned from Dr. Fisher over the last year, it was that honesty is the key to self-healing.

Lorene sat back down on the swing, and his mind began to race. No one knew the truth about that night. Trevor didn't even have the guts to tell Mr.T the truth. Should he just spill it and tell her everything?

No, he would keep it simple. He would spare Lorene the details and just tell her what she really wanted to know, "I'm not perfect, Lorene. I'm a teenager."

Lorene looked him square in the face, her expression completely serious. He waited.

"Ooooh, Boy!" She burst into laughter. "You are bad!"

She was laughing so hard, her whole body shook and half of her lemonade spilled onto the porch floor. "Lord, oh Lord! You are bad!"

Lorene's laugh was contagious and Trevor felt himself laughing alongside her. They laughed and laughed until his stomach hurt.

He didn't know if it was the relief from letting out the secret, or just feeling good about life in general, but he couldn't stop the laughter.

And he didn't want to.

ABOUT THE AUTHOR

Alex Tully lives outside Cleveland with her husband, two teenagers, and golden retriever named Trooper. *Hope for Garbage* is her debut novel.

Please consider giving a review on Amazon – it helps tremendously in getting a book noticed ☺ Thank you!!!

Visit:

www.alextullywriter.com

for more information and updates on her second novel.

40327114R00150

Made in the USA
San Bernardino, CA
16 October 2016